Praise for *A Ritchie Boy*

"Linda Kass's eagerly anticipated second novel, *A Ritchie Boy*, is an engrossing, deeply moving story of the immigrant journey, a profound and timely reminder of how refugees have woven their strengths, talents, successes, and sacrifices into the fabric of America."

—JENNIFER CHIAVERINI, *New York Times* best-selling author of *Resistance Women*

"Told as a series of interconnected stories, Linda Kass's captivating, based-in-truth novel *A Ritchie Boy* is about assimilation, hope, and perseverance."

—FOREWORD REVIEWS

"A mesmerizing kaleidoscope of stories about displacement, finding home, and the kindness of strangers. Haunting and heartfelt."

—FIONA DAVIS, national best-selling author of *The Chelsea Girls*

"I devoured *A Ritchie Boy* over a single weekend. What a rich, beautiful book Linda Kass has written. I found such poignancy and delight in every facet of these characters' lives. This is first-rate historical fiction."

—ALEX GEORGE, national and international best-selling author of *A Good American* and *The Paris Hours*

"From Vienna during the *Anschluss* to booming post-war Columbus, Linda Kass has done her homework. Half historical novel, half family saga, *A Ritchie Boy* will charm readers who loved *All the Light We Cannot See*."

—STEWART O'NAN, author of *City of Secrets*

"How did a whole generation of the Jews who were lucky enough to escape Hitler manage to reinvent themselves in America? In *A Ritchie Boy,* Linda Kass lovingly explores the spirit and the process of one such transformation. A compelling story of empathy, resilience, and the power of the American dream."

—NINA BARRETT, Owner of Bookends & Beginnings

"*A Ritchie Boy* interweaves characters from Kass's first novel, *Tasa's Song*—providing a rich context of place and perseverance during the darkness surrounding World War II. The everyday human spirit is unmasked by the revelation of profound life experiences in this engaging tale that will appeal to public library customers."

—PATRICK LOSINSKI, CEO, Columbus Metropolitan Library

"Historical fiction is a literary time machine. Thanks to the talent and imagination of Linda Kass, this journey back to the tragic days of World War II is both solemn and joyous— solemn because of the ghastly shadow of Nazism overtaking Europe, and joyous because of the forces of light that rose up to oppose it. These linked stories create a seamless and poignant whole, a deeply felt, richly described, and quietly moving meditation on faith, passion, sacrifice, struggle, and the everlasting power of family love."

—JULIA KELLER, Pulitzer Prize–winning journalist and author of *Sorrow Road: A Novel*

"Trust Linda Kass to write delicately and compassionately about the pain and bravery required of refugees. Although her milieu is the Second World War and the host country is the American Midwest, this gem of a book resonates profoundly even today."

—HELEN SCHULMAN, Author of *Come with Me*

"Linda Kass's *A Ritchie Boy* is a splendid gathering of memorable characters and stories about what it takes to leave a home, to travel to a new country, to find a way not only to survive there but to thrive. This story of persistence will warm you with its indomitable belief in family and in love."

—LEE MARTIN, author of Pulitzer Prize
finalist *The Bright Forever*

"Filled with rich historical detail and strikingly beautiful turns of phrase, this novel-in-stories moved me, inspired me, and transported me to a different time and place the way only the best tales do. Linda Kass is a masterful storyteller with a knack for taking hold of the reader's heart simply, gently, skillfully in a way that makes it easy to be swept away by her words. I highly recommend *A Ritchie Boy*."

—KRISTIN HARMEL, international best-selling author of
The Room on Rue Amélie and *The Winemaker's Wife*

"Linda Kass's *A Ritchie Boy* is an American story of World War II Jewish immigrants and a wonderful account of families that came and helped others and the communities in which they lived. Its poignant telling makes me glad that there were some happy endings from such a horrific time in history."

—LINDA WHITE, Owner of Sundog Books

"This collection of intertwined stories shines a light on the immigrant experience and their contributions winning the war. Readers of historical fiction and WWII fans will find much to admire in Linda Kass's work."

—PAMELA KLINGER-HORN, Excelsior Bay Books

A
Ritchie
Boy

A
Ritchie
Boy

A Novel

LINDA KASS

author of *Tasa's Song*

SHE WRITES PRESS

Published 2020
Printed in the United States of America
ISBN: 978-1-63152-739-5 (pbk)
ISBN: 978-1-64742-007-9 (hdcvr)
E-ISBN: 978-1-63152-740-1

Library of Congress Control Number: 2020903379

For information, address:
She Writes Press
1569 Solano Ave #546
Berkeley, CA 94707

Interior design by Tabitha Lahr

She Writes Press is a division of SparkPoint Studio, LLC.

"The Interrogation" was first published in the Winter 2019 (Vol. 35, No. 1) issue of *The MacGuffin*.

"Camp Ritchie" was first published in the June 2019 issue of *Jewish Literary Journal*.

To the memory of my father,
Ernest Stern,
a Ritchie Boy

Contents

Part Three

"We know what we are, but not what we may be."
—WILLIAM SHAKESPEARE

THE LETTER

Autumn 2016

ELI STOFF LOOKED FORWARD to Tuesdays. It was the day his family visited, en masse.

On this Tuesday in early October, the sun shining brightly into his east-facing living room, he positioned himself on his favorite armchair—the one his late wife had picked out when they decorated their condo (*after* the house and *before* the move to this twelve-hundred-square-foot apartment at the Hillside Senior Living Residences). He'd already been downstairs for breakfast, driven to Giant Eagle for Joey's banana bread, and, without his daughter's usual reprimand to slow down, made it back to his apartment with an hour to spare.

He opened *Our Souls at Night* and pulled out his bookmark. He related to the bittersweet story of a widower and a widow in advanced age coming together for companionship. His sometimes bridge partner, Elsa Katz, had filled that role for him—of course, minus the salacious twist of the novel's plot.

He liked reading fiction because it took him inside a character's mind. So much of life was about understanding human nature, he realized. He always had a novel or a biography beside him; he kept up with a half dozen magazines. If unengaged in the world around him, what point was there, after all?

He'd left his door unlocked and waited for the troupe, his hearing still strong enough to make out some distant squeals down the hallway. Today's tumultuous arrival of his grandchildren and great-grandchildren was typical—with toys pulled out of backpacks, coats strewn, greeting hugs, and excited chatter going on simultaneously. Five-year-old Roxy immediately changed into her ballerina dress and theatrically danced to Strauss's *Tales from the Vienna Woods*, a CD Eli always readied for her visit. Her little brother's eyes darted between his yellow Tonka truck and the slice of banana bread that awaited him. Roxy and Joey's twin cousins soon awakened from naps, their high-pitched cries adding to the happy mayhem.

By noon—after the twins had their diapers changed, miniature coats were matched with their little owners, toys were returned to the backpacks, and banana bread crumbs were sucked from the carpet—Eli followed the group past the furnished alcove outside his apartment and down the hall, pushing the double stroller toward the elevator. The ding of its arrival prompted goodbye kisses, the family resembling a flock of birds all pecking at once.

In the lobby, he bumped into Hannah Spring, Hillside's fortysomething activity director. "Do you have the Puccini for tonight?" Eli asked her. She assured him the DVD was in hand and that flyers had been distributed for the weekly Opera Night Eli had organized for Hillside music lovers. He'd also arranged a monthly subscription to the Columbus Symphony for a half dozen other residents. Through Hannah, he made sure a minibus was reserved for concert dates.

Marty Feldman tottered toward Eli from across the lobby. "You have a sub for this afternoon's game?" Marty asked him. "Doris has a doctor's appointment." Marty was also a widower in his nineties, the only other male bridge player among the pool of females Eli had helped assemble. Based on their skill set, it wasn't clear whether the women were interested in the game or just being in the two men's company.

Not about to get sidetracked for long, Eli assured Marty he'd found a fourth and quickly made his way to the mail room. He inserted his key, turned it, and peered into his box to find it crammed full of the usual clutter. Muttering under his breath, he immediately began purging extraneous letters, thankful to the building staff for their strategic placement of trash and recycling bins. He riffled through catalogs and bulk mailings from realtors, marketers, other retirement homes, and travel agents, pausing at a cream-colored envelope that looked like an invitation. He noticed his name handwritten in a neat script, the return address from a Holocaust museum in Farmington, Michigan. He kept this piece of mail, along with two bills, and headed upstairs to his apartment.

With the phone ringing as he approached, he pulled out his key and clumsily tried to unlock his door. He could make out classical music playing in the Cohens' next-door apartment—they turned it up because Greta was so hard of hearing—and he strained to identify the composer. *Schubert's sonata for violin and piano?* Turning the doorknob and scuffling across to the kitchen, he grabbed the phone, already agitated even before the caller greeted him. He grew weary of all the scams, with hucksters targeting old people, tricking them into divulging their bank account or credit card numbers. He'd almost learned the hard way a month back, answering detailed questions and providing his personal information until his daughter, who happened to be visiting, stopped him. After he hung up the phone, she gave him a lecture as if he were a half-wit.

"HELLO? WHO IS THIS?" He knew his voice had an edge to it. This would be the fourth crank call already today.

"Daddy? It's me. Lucy."

He felt himself starting to breathe again, his previously strained and gravelly tone turning soft and affable. "Hi, honey. Missed you this morning."

∞

AFTER IT WAS DECIDED that Lucy would come by at three after bridge, Eli situated himself at the table where Joey had devoured his banana bread just an hour earlier. Using a paper knife, he quickly opened the two bills—phone and electric—and put them aside. He treated the letter from the Holocaust museum with greater care, careful to slice the envelope while keeping it intact. As he unfolded the paper, his eyes were drawn to the salutation at the top: "Dear Ritchie Boy." His breath caught at the sight of those words, gone from his vocabulary since the war. He began to read about the planning of a reunion to be held the next summer at the Holocaust Memorial Center in Farmington Hills, Michigan. The occasion was the seventy-fifth anniversary of Camp Ritchie's opening in June of 1942.

It was in 1944 that Eli arrived there.

He folded the invitation, his old heart beating hard as a swell of memories and a flood of emotions came over him. Thinking back, at first, was like having a dream that happened to someone else. He thought how easily a man's life could slip away, so much put aside and forgotten. It seemed that in middle age, he'd had more balance. He'd remembered the past without dwelling on it, lived in the present—focusing on his family, his business obligations, his connections with his community and temple friends—and still dreamt of the future. Now, at ninety-three, he engaged fully in his present moments; there was not much future to ponder but Forest Lawn Memorial Gardens. It kept him steady and pleasant, and Eli was a practical and logical man. When his wife died last spring, he'd adjusted because that's what he'd learned to always do. He took great pleasure in his daughters and sons-in-law, their children and grandchildren. He had much and was grateful for all of it.

But now, memory beckoned him with its gentle invitation. The letter drew him backward. To Camp Ritchie, of course. But more, to how his fate had changed when he became a "Ritchie Boy." Camp Ritchie was the bridge between his lost Viennese childhood and his payment to America for his freedom. His thoughts rolled like passing clouds to his boyhood and formative friendships, to Toby and Hershel and his Army buddies.

He'd spent so little time considering that distant past, warmly enveloped inside the wonderful life he'd built for himself in America, in Ohio, with his wife and their daughters. He suddenly recalled their weekly visits to see his in-laws who'd moved to Columbus, to see his own parents—all four gone for decades. That spurred him to more recent days, to his wife's decline that prompted their move to Hillside—her short-term memory fading bit by bit, a few falls that left her more fragile and tentative. Eli settled into caring for her as he had managed all the responsibilities that had come before. He'd embraced the singular importance of the task, a renewed purpose to his life in the midst of his lengthy "third act." Then, left alone after nearly sixty-eight years of marriage, he quickly realized he needed to "reinvent" himself, as he told a close friend after Tasa's funeral.

His whole being swelled and felt hollow at once as he considered the course of his life. He pondered how, over time, his past became so blurred and distant—that particular history now gone from the physical world, only remaining in boxes of photos and letters and within his own memory. He'd kept the old albums and a few mementos in the credenza adjacent to his porch-like office space overlooking the hill from which the retirement facility took its name. He rose from his chair and, in just a couple of strides, crossed the living room to retrieve them.

He wanted to remember. It was time. The letter, somehow, made that urgent.

∞∞

LUCY SAT ON THE COUCH as Eli carried a flat and tattered cardboard box and set it down on the table in front of her. He removed the lid and pulled out an oversized leather album: a silver ship embossed at the center; a gold eagle design, its wings spread, across the top. The book was extremely old in style, worn at the edges. Inside, triangle-shaped corners held each photo, but several were missing, leaving many pictures at a slant; others were loose and would have slid out if the album were tilted. The somewhat smudged photographs, monochrome and tiny, were as creased as his hands grasping them now.

"That's my father's store in Vienna." He pointed to the photo of a European storefront showcasing his father's name in bold, black letters atop a white banner—BARTHOLOMEW STOFF—with much smaller German wording beneath. Collared shirts and trench coats filled the display windows. A hollow ache tugged at his heart as he locked his eyes on the image.

"Was it destroyed during the war?" Lucy's face bore a solemn expression as she took in each image. Eli knew she was trying to fit what seemed like pieces of a puzzle into a time and place.

So this was when you were in the ski troops in Colorado?
Was this when you were training at Camp Ritchie?
What's this coastline?

It had been years since he'd looked through this scrapbook. Now it transported him to another lifetime. As a toddler

on a sled. With his Viennese classmates. In uniform at Camp
Hale. His mother as a young woman. His Gramma Jenny.
Uncle Arthur. On furlough in Nice with his Army buddies.
With them, he was always holding a cigarette, though he'd quit
more than fifty years ago.

"That's Max Schultz, one of the GIs I trained with at
Camp Ritchie." Lucy bent forward to get a closer look, her
auburn hair falling across her face, but Eli had already moved
to the next photo, pointing. "That's my favorite of Henry
White—he was with us in Maryland too. We were all assigned
to the same military intelligence unit in France. See that impish
look on his face?"

Henry was as tall as Eli, in the same Army khakis, his cap
pushed back on his head. Eli gingerly turned each album sheet,
thick and brittle with age. There stood Henry and Eli and Max,
the three with their arms draped around each other's shoulders.
Next to it, the men were joined by two slender women with
wavy dark hair, wearing V-cut dresses.

"Ooh. Who are the ladies?"

"I don't remember. Just some gals we met up with during
furlough. That one was taken while we were still in training
in the States."

He slowly closed the tattered album, moving it aside so
they could look through his wedding book. Here the black-and-
white images were crisp, each on a full page inside a transparent
plastic slip. Each recorded by a professional. All those photos
so long ago. 1948. Sixty-eight years felt to him like yesterday.
When he and Tasa were pronounced man and wife. On the
dance floor. Cutting the cake.

Lucy turned the pages slowly and in silence, holding her
gaze on a final posed photo of her parents, outdoors in casual
clothes. She then returned to the beginning, shuffling the pages
as though looking for one particular shot. She stopped at the

image of her father the instant he stomped on a linen-wrapped glass, his face filled with intent and joy.

"Look how handsome you are, Daddy."

∞∞

MOST OF THE PHOTOGRAPHS in the wartime album were without dates or locations. But Eli knew where each was taken and when. The collection was a memento he revisited thanks to an invitation to a reunion he, at first, had no intention of attending. The organized and well-maintained wedding album he later viewed with Lucy before they went downstairs for dinner seemed like yet another lifetime, removed from his childhood and Army days. Odd, he thought, given the tight chronology: Leaving Vienna in '38, joining the Army in '43, marrying in '48.

That night, he dreamed backward. To Vienna before the *Anschluss* when Gramma Jenny still lived with them in their spare apartment in the sixteenth district. He smiled at his mother as she brought a platter of *Wiener Schnitzel* to the table. How young she looked! Toby was over for dinner, and there was talk about a ski trip. Suddenly, Eli was pleading with his mother about bringing his skis to America. Images and people flashed in and out of his unconscious mind like the films he'd seen with Hershel. At times, he found himself inside a ship at sea, then looking out the window of a fast-moving train. He was in the dream, and he was watching the dream. There were soldiers—Nazis—at a distance. He blinked and saw himself wearing an Army uniform. Surrounded by his Camp Ritchie buddies: Max, Henry, Bobby Saltman. Time didn't make sense. Where was he? Mountains were covered in glistening snow, and he was laughing until another scene took its place, one in which he sat in a stark room conducting an interrogation. These impressions blurred and morphed from one person and place to another. He was playing bridge with Hershel one moment, listening to jazz with Toby the next. There was Zelda Muni, John Brandeis, Arthur. His parents were still alive. Tasa was still alive, pressed in next to him.

Much of the detail faded when Eli woke, although the vague residue of his dream left him foggy, unsettled. One memory remained fixed: that of frozen farmland slipping past parted curtains of a train window. He considered how the frosty field flickered rapidly past him, much like the nearly eight decades had since his boyhood ski trip in the Austrian Alps. He tried to get past this reverie and move into his day, one that passed, on the surface, much like the one before—breakfast with friends, a quick trip to the grocery, calls from his daughters, a game of bridge, an evening with music and a book. Hour by hour, though, he kept imagining going to Michigan and joining up with his MI buddies, not even sure which were still alive and if they'd be physically capable of making the trip next summer. Or if he would be around by then.

By dusk, Eli gazed out his office window, lulled by the hypnotic ticking of the clock on his desk. All that remained of the light was an orange glaze on the western horizon.

Part One

SKIING IN TYROL

March 1938

SNOW HAD BEGUN TO fall as the train pulled out from the Wien Sudbahnhof station. It continued steadily through the morning, thickening over the countryside until there was no edge to the land where it met the chalky sky. A series of fast-moving frozen images floated past Toby's window. He caught a glimpse of a farmhouse and an old oak tree. Then open terrain.

Despite the rhythmic vibration, Toby couldn't help fidgeting in his seat. He felt hot in his heavy wool sweater. And his stomach growled. The ham sandwich his mother had packed him was in his rucksack in the overhead bin. To get to it, he'd have to climb over Eli.

He looked over at his childhood friend who was fast asleep. Eli Stoff lived in his apartment building. They'd attended *Volksschule* together since they were six, were both accepted into the *Gymnasium* in their Vienna neighborhood. They were like brothers: Eli taking the role of protector, keeping Toby out of trouble, and pushing him to engage more in school activities.

The long train ride gave Toby plenty of time to consider how he found himself heading to the western province of Tyrol with—other than Eli—eight boys he disliked. He would have rather spent these two days doing almost anything but skiing in the frigid cold. He could still be in bed, reading Kafka's *The Trial* that his father had lent him or, better yet, listening to jazz on his parents' phonograph.

He'd told Eli as much when their teacher, Herr Bohm, first announced the class outing. He reminded Eli he didn't even own a pair of skis. His lack of interest in the national pastime set Toby apart as a contrarian, but he didn't care. "Come on, don't be a spoilsport," Eli had chided him. "I have an old set you can borrow. Other stuff too."

His friend's prodding hadn't really persuaded him. It was what had been brewing at school, an undercurrent of tension that gnawed at Toby all year. It came to a head last December when two students approached him and Eli in the cafeteria.

"Hey there, Stoff. You took my seat. Think you own this space?" The bigger of the two boys, Bruno Maurer, had seemed eager to stir things up. His black eyes narrowed when he spoke; his voice bellowed. Franz Haider, stout with a mop of blond hair, plunked down on the wooden bench and slid his tray across the table hard enough to spill the water glass onto Eli.

Eli took his napkin and sopped up the liquid, his voice controlled, unperturbed. "This table is all yours, fellas. We were just leaving." Eli motioned for Toby to get up, his expression hovering between resignation and puzzlement. As he stepped away, he said, "Enjoy your lunch," without even a faint trace of sarcasm.

Toby remembered his own rage as if it were yesterday. Eli was sturdy and broad-shouldered and could have posed a threat to the roughnecks. When they were out of earshot, he had asked Eli why he didn't stand up to them. It wouldn't work, was all Eli replied. "They'll just keep at it. Up the ante."

While he was thankful not to be the butt of jokes or ploys, as were Eli and the other Jewish kids, he burned with humiliation on his friend's behalf. Eli never let on how he felt. Toby watched Eli calmly deflect every confrontation so it wouldn't escalate. He gave Eli a lot of credit for his self-control. Meanwhile, he bore enough worry and angst for the both of them.

"Approaching Kitzbühel Hahnenkamm." He felt the train slowing as Herr Bohm's booming voice rang through the confined space. "Collect your belongings, boys."

Eli stretched his long legs in the cramped space and stifled a yawn. "How long was I asleep?"

"Two hours. You were really great company." Toby climbed over Eli into the aisle, retrieving his soggy ham sandwich. "At least you didn't snore."

Toby shoved the last bite in his mouth as the whistle announced their arrival. He closed the flap on his bag and grabbed the borrowed ski gear. The rail guard unlatched the door and moved aside while passengers scrambled past him onto the platform. Toby followed Eli down the aisle. When he reached the opening, a thick smoke sprayed up from the train's chimney like a cloud of steam. A hissing noise cut across the crisp ether. Just as Eli was about to step down, Toby felt himself being shoved from behind and he pitched forward against him. Eli lost his footing and fell to his knees, but he sprang back up and brushed the snow off his pants.

"Hey!" Toby spun around and found himself face-to-face with Rudy Kraus. "Take it easy."

"Relax, Wermer." Rudy smirked. "I didn't mean anything."

Toby knew better. "So, you're just naturally clumsy?"

The remaining boys piled out, some jumping two-footed onto the icy ground. A few jabbed playfully at their nearest classmates. Excited voices glazed the cold air with a frosty mist.

Herr Bohm instructed them to line up along the platform to take the roll. "Christoph Eisler, Stefan Frece, Rolland Gerg . . ."

Slapped by a gust of wind, Toby pulled down the earflaps on his cap and waited for his name to be called, last as always. Everything about this trip bothered him. Labeled "optional" since students were responsible for the train fare and overnight fee at the youth hostel, it discouraged participation from working-class families. : And the trip was scheduled on a March weekend when Jewish classmates observed their Sabbath, instead of during the week of winter break.

". . . Franz Haider, Rudolf Kraus, Karl Langer, Bruno Maurer . . ."

Toby glared at the pair of ruffians who'd taunted Eli months back—Bruno the instigator, Franz his lackey. Along with Rudy, they injected threat and intolerance into a school culture where Jews were in the minority. In the class of twenty, there were only two—Eli, and Freidel Shamansky. Freidel had passed on the trip. Eli's family was more secular, and Eli insisted on going, perhaps the rebel in him striking back against the bad guys. Eli's mother at first cautioned both boys about taking the trip because of the steep slopes and possible icy conditions. But at last night's dinner, she urged them to stay watchful given the "mood" of the times.

". . . Dietrich Rauch, Eli Stoff, Tobias Wermer."

"Look where we are!" Eli whispered the words to Toby, his face shining.

He pointed beyond the train station, which bisected the village of Kitzbühel. Toby took in the mountain flanks sur-rounding them. They stood deep in the valley of this medieval town with its buttressed walls, as if on the floor of a giant amphitheater chiseled out of the earth.

Following Herr Bohm's even pace, the boys marched down the narrow, cobbled main road, the snow squeaking under their feet. They passed hostelries, cafés, and taverns with hand-drawn signs, until they reached their lodgings. Toby stared up at the frescoes of double-headed eagles on the lobby ceiling as his teacher assigned roommates, predictably placing Toby and Eli together. Bohm told them to unpack their things, change clothes, and meet back downstairs in half an hour.

The room was large and comfortable with big windows, through which the sun's reflection off the snow streamed into the chamber. Squinting, Toby plopped on the bed, its surface overlaid with a feather coverlet. "Can you believe this? We're almost on our own!"

"You sound like you're finally happy to be on this trip." Eli's broad smile softened the deep cleft in his chin. "Ready to hit the Alps?"

Toby held his tongue rather than express his true preference—to stay in the hostel and warm himself by the fireplace in the lounge. Eli was already pulling out their ski trousers, boots, mittens, and caps. Toby tightened his suspenders to keep the trousers taut as Eli had instructed. Even though Eli's hand-me-downs were from years earlier, they looked baggy on Toby's short, thin frame. He tucked the pant legs into the tops of his boots—ankle-high and uncomfortable.

∞∞∞

THE SNOWFALL HAD FINALLY LET UP. Under the cobalt sky, the boys faced an endless series of mountain peaks still warm from the sun, the snow deep and powdery in spots. They headed for the slopes, carrying their wooden skis in one hand, the bamboo poles in the other. Herr Bohm had divided the students into two groups. The teacher took six and assigned Eli, the best skier in the class, the responsibility for the remaining three: Toby, Franz Haider, and Karl Langer. Toby was pleased. Separating

Franz from Bruno and including Karl—the most agreeable of their classmates—might help the four to get along.

After they clamped on their skis, the boys began the slow work of traversing up the mountain trails. Toby stabbed his pole in the ground, sliding his opposite leg forward as he propelled himself upward. His heart pounding, he sucked in deep breaths until his throat became raw and dry. Eli slowed his pace, letting the small group catch up to him. Grateful for the brief respite, Toby regarded his three classmates. Only their cheeks were exposed, reddened from the frigid air and revealing traces of downy new facial hair.

"Let's hike toward the Streif to get a better view." The frozen moisture on Eli's lips cracked. His teeth chattered as he spoke. "Then we'll head for slopes we can ski."

Toby didn't care much about this legendary ski run, although he wasn't clueless about all the Olympic champions who had competed here. He tried to follow Karl's measured strides while eyeing the rolling moguls obstructing his view. Once he got his bearings, he had to admit the trek was invigorating. Beads of perspiration trickled down his back. He pulled off his hat and, realizing his typically unkempt hair was matted up with sweat, shoved it back on his head. He may not have been in the best condition to battle the climb, but at least he wasn't overweight like Franz, who was struggling to keep up.

"Wait up!" A voice rang out behind them. It was Rudy.

Toby locked eyes with Eli and mouthed, *Trouble*. Eli shrugged and shortened his steps to allow Rudy to catch up.

"Heading to the Streif?" Rudy was breathless, each word pushing frost into the space between the boys.

Eli nodded. "Just close enough to see it. Then we'll find tows for some easy runs. Bohm okay with you leaving his group?"

Rudy gave a thumbs-up, and the five continued their steady march in near silence but for Franz's grunting when the incline grew steeper. They built a meditative rhythm that kept them equidistant from one another, picking up speed as the terrain flattened. Their path narrowed between two rows of trees, the snow a fresh powder barely packed down by the skis of others. Puffs of cloud drifted in the indigo sky as they trudged toward Hahnenkamm, the mountain enormous before them.

Toby felt almost lightheaded and wasn't sure if it was the altitude, the physical strain of the climb, or the awesome sight in front of him. Wide-open slopes blanketed in white were flecked with evergreens that blurred into a maze of ridges. Rays of sun fell through the tall trees like cathedral light.

Arriving at a midpoint where the summit came into clear view, the four classmates encircled Eli and stopped, fixing their poles into the snow, stretching their necks to take in the mammoth pinnacle in all its splendor. As they continued to stare at the panorama, their silence felt peaceful to Toby as if, for that moment, the boys were of like minds.

He wasn't sure how long they stood there spellbound before Eli summoned them to move on. A biting wind sent a shiver through Toby's body.

∞∞O

IT WAS MIDAFTERNOON BY the time they reached gentler slopes. Toby clutched the old-fashioned rope tow but could barely hang on to it at first. The line was stiff and icy. It took all five skiers to steady and balance it. On his second try, he was jerked off his feet when he grasped the cord too quickly. When he fell, he nearly dragged all of them down into the snow.

"Look, guys, I'm a clod. You'd do better if I headed back to the hostel."

"We're in this together, Wermer, even if you do ski like my little sister." Karl used his mitten to wipe his runny nose.

"I'd say Ida skis better than Toby," Franz added as he nudged Rudy, and the boys began laughing.

Toby felt the camaraderie despite being the butt of their fun.

"I've got an idea. Follow me," Eli announced. He led the way and before long they found newer lifts—contraptions with continuously circulating overhead wire ropes that could carry the skier.

"I gotta say, you know these slopes, Stoff." Karl grabbed a horizontal bar coming around the drum wheel, and it immediately pulled him forward as it lifted him upward. "Wow, this is easy."

Toby seized the next bar in line, not wanting to look like a sissy. In no time, they were pulled to the summit. Eli was the first to shove off, followed by Rudy, wild-eyed as he sped down the slope. Franz and Karl took off side by side. The four returned to the top of the run while Toby was still trying to find his nerve to take the plunge.

"Go into a deep tuck," Eli said, standing close to Toby. He softened his voice. "Don't worry, the worst that can happen is you'll fall. And you'll stop at the bottom." He shot Toby a wink as the others chuckled.

Toby pushed off with his poles and tried to remember all of Eli's instructions—keep his knees flexed, separate his skis for greater stability, edge the skis in an icy traverse, weight-shift to stay balanced, stem-turn to slow his descent. The initial stretch was the steepest, so he instinctively edged both knees into a snowplow position and didn't look down. His heartbeat felt like a drum pattern in triple time when he slid through an ice skid and fought to stay upright. Getting through the near mishap boosted his confidence, and he picked up speed from there until he skidded, unsteadily, to a stop.

The boys attempted a couple of runs on a new slope though the daylight was fading. Dark clouds had formed overhead, the late afternoon sky taking on the color of a bruise. As they headed back, Eli stopped in his tracks. "Look! An alpine chamois!"

The goat-antelope was several ski lengths ahead of them. It looked fully grown, probably fifty kilograms and about seventy centimeters tall. The animal's horns were short and straight, hooked backward near the tip. Toby had never seen a chamois this close.

"It's a male," Eli added.

"How would you know, Stoff?" Rudy glowered at Eli. "Or maybe you're an expert since your people sacrificed goats, right?"

Toby stabbed his poles into the frozen earth, considering a riposte to Rudy's affront. Before he could think of a comeback, Karl elbowed Franz.

"Maybe he checked out the size of his balls, lamebrain." The two boys snorted in laughter.

"I saw a herd of chamois once before. Read about them afterward." Eli continued to watch the animal, ignoring the mockery. "The horn of the male is thicker. That's how you tell them apart."

Rudy narrowed his eyes and observed Eli, like he was sizing him up. Toby wondered if Eli's calm and detachment provoked Rudy further. Or if it would shut him down. The goat's hooves made a crunching sound as it took a few steps in the snow. Toby noticed black markings below the animal's eyes and imagined it a fearless opponent.

"Let's get closer. Surround it," Rudy suggested. The rest of them stood still, watching Rudy lurch toward the mountain goat, then stumble. At that instant, the chamois sped away, jumping high moguls with ease.

Toby had the urge to taunt Rudy but restrained himself. He felt a whirl of wind and watched a mass of snow lift in front of them. He pulled his earflaps low, tightened his scarf, and, with the help of his poles, pivoted in the direction of Kitzbühel.

∞∞

TOBY FELT SLUGGISH AND famished after the day's exertion. Except for Bruno, the other ski group dispersed to their rooms or down the street with Herr Bohm. He couldn't understand why any of them would want to leave the warmth of the fire-place or the tub of hot apple cider the hostel's owner was ladling into mugs. Before long, the boys who'd stayed back were all sitting around the central fireplace, tossing potatoes wrapped in foil into the embers and tasting a variety of hard and soft cheeses brought up from the cellar.

"I faced down a wild mountain creature," Rudy told the group. He took a gulp of cider and wiped his mouth with the back of his hand. "Scared him off."

Toby rolled his eyes. "I'm not sure how wild that goat was. Seemed pretty tame if you ask me."

"Yeah, you were the wild one, Rudy." Franz turned to Bruno. "Anything interesting go down in your group?"

Bruno carefully peeled the foil off his potato and took a bite. He grimaced and spat the chunk on the floor. "*Ach, mein Gott!* This is too hot to eat!" He set the potato down and turned to Franz. "Stefan and Dietrich were showing off. Plowed right in front of Herr Bohm. First time I saw the man so rankled."

"Anyone get hurt?" Toby's legs ached. He stood up to stretch.

"Stefan skipped over a crusty patch and turned his ankle." Bruno popped a huge chunk of cheese in his mouth, his cheeks puffing out, but he kept talking. "Bohm ended up taking him back here to ice it. That's when we started having some fun."

Toby walked closer to the hearth. The heat felt good. He held his hands up to the fire, rubbing them together. The day hadn't been that bad after all. He'd learned how to ski, seen the most awesome mountain in Austria, even gotten close to a mountain goat. There was the insolence of Rudy, but it had been safely contained. He was now ready to put his feet up and enjoy himself.

Voices and a burst of laughter returned his attention to his classmates. Just outside the banter, Eli sat quietly, holding his mug of hot cider with both hands, blowing across its surface before taking a sip.

As Toby turned back toward the fireplace, his eyes locked on a wooden gramophone with a brass horn tucked into the corner beyond the hearth. "Hey, look over here!" He dashed over and opened the cabinet, his eyes widening at the records stacked neatly in vertical slits. He knelt down and looked closer. Benny Goodman. Count Basie. Duke Ellington. "Wow, incredible."

"Let's play this one." Franz grabbed Ellington's "It Don't Mean a Thing." "My cousin lives in Hamburg and goes to clubs, where there's wild dancing to all this up-tempo music."

"Yeah, I heard about those swing clubs. Makes the girls go crazy." Bruno shuffled through several albums while Toby slid the Duke Ellington out of its jacket, delicately placing the needle onto the groove. A fiddle, then piano backed by a full orchestra, blasted into the lounge. *It don't mean a thing if you ain't got that swing. It don't mean a thing, all you gotta do is swing.*

Toby couldn't make out all the words, but it didn't matter because of the steady pulse. Franz moved his head up and down to the beat, his hair falling into his face. *It makes no difference if it's sweet or hot. Just give that rhythm everything you've got.*

"This stuff's good, actually." Rudy started tapping his feet. All the boys surrounded the phonograph. "My dad calls it Negro noise. Boy, would he whack me up and down for listening to this."

Toby had heard the Kraus family was pretty reactionary, that Herr Kraus could be cruel in disciplining his son. Maybe that explained Rudy's brash and malicious behavior. "Let me see some of these."

Toby took the records from Bruno, excited by the gems at his fingertips. A Django Reinhardt. Count Basie's "One O'Clock Jump." Some slower Ellington tunes—"Mood Indigo," "In a Sentimental Mood"—along with "Sophisticated Lady" and "Caravan."

"Let's put on Benny Goodman," Eli said as he looked over Toby's shoulder. "You have this one at home, Toby." He pointed to "Sing, Sing, Sing."

"I love the clarinet in that piece." Toby rested the needle on the record. "Listen to the drums, the trumpets. There's nothing like this sound."

The boys settled back in their chairs, bouncing along with the drum solos. Toby pretended he had sticks in his hand, flicking his wrists with the beat. He looked over at Eli, whose eyes were closed, his shoulders swaying from side to side. Rudy, Bruno, Franz—all of them were caught up in the pulsating tempo. Toby held back an amused grin. They were listening to a Jewish bandleader, something only Eli would know. He certainly wasn't about to clue in the others.

∞∞

"I'LL ADMIT WE ALL had some good moments together. But Rudy—I just can't trust that guy." Toby's words filled the darkness of their room that night.

A long silence followed, and Toby thought Eli had fallen asleep until he answered. "He's just a bully. That's all he is. But Franz, Karl, and the others keep him in check."

Toby sat up in disbelief. "Only a bully? You heard what he said about the music. 'Negro noise.' And how he insulted you as a Jew earlier. It's how he's been brought up, don't you see? It's what he believes." His eyes began adjusting to the dark. "People like that scare me, and they should scare you."

"Come on. Lighten up. You're blowing all this out of proportion." Eli pulled the covers tightly under his chin and rolled away from Toby. "Stop being a worrywart."

With that, Eli dozed off and didn't so much as stir again. Despite his exhaustion, Toby felt like he tossed and turned all night. He woke up still fatigued, enough that he begged off joining the others for an early morning trek. After packing, he waited in the hostel lobby until the last of his classmates trounced down the steps lugging their bags and skis.

Standing on the station platform, he could feel the day's heat penetrate his face despite the frigid temperature. The sun stood high in the cerulean sky, like a large ball of crystal with shimmering spikes. As he took a final rapt look at his surroundings, a whistle in the distance startled him, the sound stirring a foreboding he couldn't explain. The train's outline came into view. Picking up his bag, he followed Franz, Bruno, and Karl toward the nearest car, where the conductor waved them inside.

"All the way in the back!" The rail man pointed toward the exit door.

"I'm right behind you." Eli patted Toby's shoulder.

Toby stepped on board and grabbed two empty seats while Eli hoisted their bags onto the overhead rack. As the door slammed shut, Toby settled in, staring out the window's thick glass. The train began rolling down the track, slowly at first, then gathering speed.

"This is how fast I flew down those mountains this morning," Bruno barked out from behind, where he sat with Franz.

"Or maybe like that mountain goat as he bolted from Rudy's clutches." Franz hit the back of Toby's seat, laughing.

"Well, at least I tried to do something, Haider." Sitting on the aisle seat across from Bruno, Rudy leaned over toward Franz. "But you just stood there while Stoff analyzed the goat's sex. Oh, excuse me, Stoff. The 'chamois.'"

"Cut it out, Kraus. Let's just have a peaceful ride, okay?" Toby said. He'd wanted to sound more commanding, but his words came out pleading.

"I don't need a little creep like you telling me what to do, Wermer."

Toby let the comment go. His muscles ached. He tried to take in the scenery, but his eyelids drooped as the fast-moving images blurred. The repetitive sounds of the train lulled him into a stupor.

He awoke abruptly to the screeching of metal and the steam whistle's shrill cry. He looked out the window and realized they were approaching a station. He yawned, stretching his arms above his head, then elbowed Eli. "Where are we?"

"Salzburg, I think."

Relief washed over Toby. He must have slept for several hours. They were almost home. Maybe he had been overreacting, as Eli had suggested.

Just then, Rudy jumped out of his seat. "Look at all the soldiers!" His outburst rose above the clanging bells as the train eased to a stop.

Eli stretched across Toby, and the two stared out the window. The sound of cheering erupted. Eli's voice was barely audible but somber. "Now it begins."

Hundreds of soldiers with Nazi banners and swastikas surrounded the depot and loading platform. Toby turned back and saw Rudy's eyes widening, saw all of his classmates transfixed on the scene.

"Students! Stay put. We still have another stop at Linz before we arrive in Vienna." Herr Bohm held onto a metal bar to steady himself, his voice strident over the clamor outside the train.

Rudy stood up, edging into the aisle. "The Germans will save Austria!"

"Are you crazy?" Toby's words rushed out before he could stop himself.

Rudy stepped toward Toby's and Eli's seats. "Some people
. . ." He glared down at Eli. "Some people have sucked our
country dry. Hitler will change that."

Toby's entire body tensed up. Until this moment, all of
Rudy's taunts of Eli had been like small jabs—those of a thug,
but without the power of a political movement behind him.
Now Rudy was making a slur on Eli's family, a misguided one
at that. The Stoffs were far from wealthy. Eli's mother was an
English language tutor; his father owned a small company that
made uniforms.

Toby looked over at Eli, whose head was down, his hands
folded on his lap. A flood of compassion washed over him, then
a wave of anger. He took in a breath to measure his words. He
felt protected by their teacher, but speaking out in defense of
Jews exposed him to classmates who probably saw the world as
Rudy did, or were starting to. Their silence seemed to confirm
this. "Austria's problems—like Germany's—have to do with
the Great War, not Jewish—"

"What world are you living in? My parents say our Austrian
dictatorship has given a pass to Jews like your buddy here."

An undercurrent of whispers swept through the train car.

Toby stood, stretching across Eli as he glared into Rudy's
eyes. "Then why don't you run out there and sign up before
it's too late?"

Rudy raised a hand as if to hit Toby. Eli jumped out of
his seat, pushed past Toby, and grabbed Rudy's arm in midair.

"Get your hands off me, Jew boy!" Rudy tried to swing at
Eli with his other arm, but Eli grabbed that one, too, and held fast.

"You don't scare me, Kraus. Are you so weak that you
have to attack someone smaller?" Eli scowled at Rudy, not
moving and not easing up on his grip. Suddenly Rudy rammed
Eli with his body, and for a moment, Eli's hold on him loosened. But before Rudy could strike, Eli threw a punch at his

jaw, knocking Rudy backward so he fell onto Bruno's lap. Eli's face was expressionless as he watched Rudy awkwardly pull himself up. Toby stood gaping, horrified.

"Eli, Rudolf! Break it up." Herr Bohm's face reddened as he bounded down the aisle and inserted his body between the two. The imposing teacher took hold of Rudy's shoulders and pressed him into his seat, whispering something in his ear. Then he pivoted toward Eli, addressing him in a low voice that Toby could also hear. "Your friend is making things difficult. His outspoken tongue will get you into deep trouble."

Bohm turned toward Toby, a black look on his face. "There are battles that can't be won. Look what your provocation just created for your Jewish friend here."

Toby stood there clenching his fists. Eli locked eyes with him, motioning his head toward their seats. Toby eased himself down and turned sullenly toward the window just as the train started coasting out of the station. He felt the beat of the train's wheels, solemn like drums. As he watched the Alps recede in the distance, a flicker of yesterday's thrill sparkled back in him. He thought of how the grandeur of the mountains had brought a bunch of fifteen-year-olds together. And how they were about to be split apart.

ZELDA'S GAMBLE

April 1938

ZELDA PAUSED AT THE third landing of her fifth-floor walk-up, switching the sack of groceries to her other hip. At the top of the final flight, she found her apartment door ajar and caught Giorgio's head peeking into the hallway. He reached for her bag and gave her a quick kiss. "Your day okay?"

She offered a tilt of her head, raising an eyebrow. Hard to call any day cleaning toilets at the Waldorf a good one. She tossed her wool coat aside and nudged Giorgio into the kitchen. "One guest left me a dollar with a kind note, so we have him to thank for our dinner."

"I got the night off. Let me do the cooking." Giorgio laid the pappardelle and Roma tomatoes on the counter, then pulled out a saucepan. He turned to her, catching her gaze. "You got a letter from Lila." From the stack of mail on the kitchen table, he plucked the top envelope and handed it to her.

From Lila? Her breath caught in her throat. She looked at the sloping script of her name addressed on the onionskin envelope, the elegance of the *Z* and the *M*: *Zelda Muni.* The same graceful penmanship Lila perfected in *Gymnasium*, where they met as girls, and which she marshaled for her letters to Zelda, now that an immense ocean separated the two.

Zelda walked into the living room and eased herself into their rickety armchair. It had been months since she'd heard from her friend. The heavy mood of Lila's last letter reminded Zelda of their adolescence in Vienna, when rationing and lessons from the Great War replaced the gaiety of the Vienna Fasching, when they learned to waltz in open-air squares. Back then the two were inseparable. Like sisters. They could complete each other's sentences. The ink was barely dry on the Treaty of Versailles when they began their studies at the University of Vienna filled with big ideas and plans—Zelda's dream to someday become an art curator, Lila's to be an English professor. Lila ended up teaching English to children because it seemed like more important work. She was always looking out for everyone else. Zelda reminded herself that every major decision in her life, including marrying Giorgio and immigrating with him to America, was done with Lila's input and blessing.

Her fingers tore at the flap. As she scanned Lila's words, her gut tightened. She'd read the newspapers. Or thought she'd read them. More likely she just stared at the newsprint, too consumed with her own miseries and failures since she and Giorgio arrived in New York to concentrate. The miscarriages. The job humiliations. Their worthless degrees. The daily indignities. Their powerlessness. Some days she felt like screaming. But now her rage was about Lila's plight.

On Friday, a pack of hooligans attacked Eli on his way home from school, forced him onto his hands and knees, made him scrub the pavement while they spat on him . . .

Zelda folded the letter, pushed off from the chair, and hurried back to the kitchen. "They have to get out—Lila, Bart, and their son. They have to get out of Vienna."

"What are we supposed to do?" Giorgio gave her that look, the one she called "The Wall." She remembered when his face used to be open and sunny, when he was receptive and eager, his deep brown eyes gentle. Years of six-day stints waiting tables for three dollars a shift had taken its toll. Unspoken was the reality that his engineering skills had grown stale, along with his precious diploma.

In truth, they'd both hardened. She didn't want to admit or confront it. She kept telling herself things would get better, that some opportunity would open up. Maybe they'd soon be able to afford a better apartment. But they continued to bump against the low ceiling of possibilities for immigrants in their new country. Their lives had become stagnant. She saw that now as she felt a stirring, a call to action.

She sat down at the kitchen table, talking to Giorgio's back as he chopped vegetables. "We *must* help her family get affidavits. They need someone respectable to vouch for them."

"And who might you suggest?"

"Don't be sarcastic with me, Giorgio."

He turned to face her, this time his gaze intent. "I want to help Lila too, but we are barely making ends meet." He shook his head, his voice breaking. "And look what would be awaiting them."

"Our lives aren't so bad." She stood up and pulled him toward her. "We have each other." Holding him tightly, she added quietly, "At least we *have* jobs . . . and we have our freedom. We can't ever forget that."

"You're right . . . I'm sorry." Neither spoke as they moved apart. His face softened. "What about Giuseppe?"

"Just because he owns the restaurant . . ." Zelda's words trailed off. The people they knew were immigrants, too—hardworking, struggling. And there were quotas, especially for Jews. Immigration officers wanted assurances that the potential émigré could find work and not become a public drain.

"What about someone at the Waldorf?" Giorgio shut off the faucet and reached for a towel.

She considered that possibility. But her immediate boss was a Mexican who reported to a second-generation Russian Jew. No one they knew measured up any better. Guido and his wife, Sophie, lived in the apartment below, and through them they'd met Sophie's brother and his wife—a Macy's stockroom worker and a hotel maid, like Zelda.

"We need to find someone financially independent. Established. Someone born here," Zelda replied. Her eyes filled with tears. "Someone who will vouch for a family unknown to them."

"There's got to be someone." Giorgio blotted Zelda's cheeks with the dish towel. "Now, now. Where's the Zelda I met in Zug, the girl who could corner any mogul in her path?"

∞∞∞

SHE WAS CAREFUL NOT to wake Giorgio the next morning, remembering he had late hours at the restaurant for the next four nights. Saturday was her day for errands. She gathered her clothing—a crimson blouse and navy skirt—and tiptoed to the bathroom, where she dressed and then contemplated her image in the mirror. How this outfit contrasted with her maid's uniform! The white-collared black smock with its double-breasted rows of silver buttons had begun to define her, smother her. Coupled with her accented English, it guaranteed the hotel guests—even her coworkers—could only see her as an immigrant servant.

Now, as she examined her reflection, she felt a flicker of purpose and wondered what happened to the person Lila no doubt still believed she was writing to. Her mind drifted to twelve years earlier, after she and Giorgio first got to New

York and settled on the Lower East Side, in their Mott Street apartment: her first big job interview.

"Do you like the tan suit, or would the navy dress be more . . . proper?" Zelda had flitted back and forth from her closet, holding up one outfit after another for Giorgio's reaction.

"You look beautiful—and professional—in both." Giorgio propped up his bed pillows and leaned toward her. "Come closer. Let me have a better look."

Zelda frowned. "Please take me seriously, Giorgio. No one else seems to."

It had been a bright spring morning, just like this one, and Zelda recalled her optimism as she introduced herself to the Met's director of impressionist collections. Her work as curator at the Vienna Künstlerhaus made her eminently qualified, but the director had given her only a tight smile as Zelda struggled to find the correct English words to describe her breadth of experience.

Even now Zelda's face colored with anger as she remembered her loss of dignity. The heels of her boots echoed down the steps of her building. She was heading for Stern Brothers, where she'd seen an advertisement of a closeout sale on recliners. It was time to replace their tired armchair before it collapsed under one of their weights. Maybe the excursion would help her think through a way to help Lila.

She pressed her body against the wooden door until it finally gave way, a burst of brisk air slapping her face. She set out at a fast clip past workmen and mothers with strollers, nearly bumping into a man with a tin cup as she approached the entrance of the Ninth Avenue el. She got out five cents for the fare and took the train uptown to Forty-Second Street, exiting on Fifth Avenue across from Bryant Park, the sun temporarily blinding her. Straight ahead was the New York Public Library, its stately entry columns reminding her of Vienna's Burgtheater, where Beethoven premiered his first symphony. Where she and Lila had spent most Sunday afternoons.

She crossed the street and walked a block north. At Stern Brothers, an impeccably appointed doorman in white gloves and a top hat greeted her. She slipped through the revolving glass doors, almost carried into the store's marble lobby. The whirl of activity—shoppers darting in every direction—disoriented her for an instant.

Moments after she stepped off the motor stair on the seventh floor, she spotted a brown leather recliner among the many armchairs filling the showroom. She plunked herself into its thick cushioned seat and found it had a footrest that rose up with a lever. She turned over the tag, surprised to find such an affordable price. After the salesman took her order and she made delivery arrangements, she wandered the aisles, admiring rows of kitchenware and bedding that came to a dead end at the elevator.

She stared up at the black arrow that inched clockwise as the elevator ascended, stopping at the Roman numeral two before it stuck at three for several minutes. Contemplating whether to wait or head back for the motor stair, she glanced at the framed descriptions of merchandise offered on each of Stern Brothers' nine floors. Her eyes strayed to a plaque describing the store's mission, history, and ownership. It said the store was founded in the nineteenth century by the sons of Jewish immigrants, that the family had run it for decades. It described their commitment to community stewardship, their philanthropy. The current executive in charge of all operations was a man named John Brandeis.

A vague thought, like an unformed cloud, floated by. Zelda didn't attempt to shape its meaning, but when the elevator's tall brass doors opened, she stepped inside and impulsively pushed the button marked "B" for the executive offices.

As the elevator finally jerked to her stop, the doors opened into a plush reception foyer. A young receptionist sat upright behind a dark oak desk. She wore a high-necked cream blouse, her strawberry blond hair pulled back into a tight bun. The door to an office on the right was closed. The gold plate on it was engraved: *John E. Brandeis.*

"Excuse me. I'd like to know if Mr. Brandeis might be available?"

"Mr. Brandeis doesn't work on Saturdays."

Of course. This was the Sabbath. It had been so long since she and Lila spent every waking moment together, she'd almost forgotten the basic customs of her friend's religion. Although Lila herself didn't always follow them, she would've rolled her eyes at Zelda's lapse.

"I understand. But is there a time I could see him this coming week?"

"And who are you?"

Without thinking, Zelda blurted, "A friend of the family."

The receptionist glanced up at Zelda quizzically. She lowered her eyes to the open calendar book on her desk as she pronounced, "He's an extremely busy man." Licking her index finger, she began to comb through several pages filled with crisp handwriting. She closed the book with a smack. "I can't get you in to see him for at least a month, and then—"

"Oh, no." Zelda's voice quavered. "That's too late!"

"Madam. I don't know who you are, and I suspect neither does Mr. Brandeis." The woman pursed her lips and glared at Zelda. "Can't you direct your issue to one of our store managers?"

Zelda felt her face getting hot.

I am no longer sought even as a private English tutor. They are taking away our freedoms—our humanity—bit by bit. We desperately need a safe haven!

"No, I can't." Zelda placed her hands on the desk and leaned closer to the receptionist, her gaze steady as she spoke. "Only Mr. Brandeis can help. The purpose of my business is urgent—it's a life-and-death matter."

The young woman's stoic face rearranged itself as she appraised Zelda once again. "Please, madam. Aren't you being a little dramatic?"

"There are people . . ." Zelda could hear her heart pounding in her ears. She glanced about the office, letting the seconds pass while her mind slowed down. She took a deep breath and slowly exhaled before she returned her fixed attention to the receptionist. "There are people Mr. Brandeis knows who are under immediate threat. He will want to be apprised of this. I have that information."

"What is your name?"

"Zelda. Z-e-l-d-a. Muni. M-u-n-i."

"All right, Zelda Muni. You're putting me in a difficult position . . ." The woman gave Zelda a studied look. "I may regret doing this . . . but I'll get you in during Mr. Brandeis's lunch hour next Wednesday. At noon. And don't be a minute late."

"Thank you! Thank you so much. I'm most appreciative." Zelda backed away from the desk and hurried to the elevator.

In the lobby, she almost bumped into the man who'd greeted her earlier.

"Did you get what you needed, ma'am?"

Zelda flashed him a smile, but she was already past him, propelled toward the revolving glass doors.

She instinctively walked toward the library. When she first moved to New York, she'd spent hours in its Main Reading Room, discovering rare German works on art theory among its thousands of volumes. Heading straight for the reference section, she passed floor-to-ceiling shelves of current magazines. A photograph caught her eye from the cover of *Life*—a German soldier blowing a bugle. She riffled through the pages until she got to the story about Hitler taking over Austria. Pictured were a group of Nazis, their right arms raised in a salute while singing; the caption noted it was the Party anthem, "Die Fahne Hoch." On the next page was a photo of blond, full-faced boys in Nazi uniforms with Hitler shaking their hands, their eyes shining. This was her homeland, where Lila was right now.

Nazi authorities stormed into Bart's uniform store. They grabbed his two associates by the necks and literally threw them outside into the street. They shouted obscenities at Bart, told him they were taking over. Who treats people this way, Zelda?

She flung the magazine back where she found it and marched to the stack of wooden drawers against the far wall. She flipped the white index cards, scanning for "Brandeis," then moved to the next drawer until the titles began to blur. She finally located several articles and a quiet corner to read them. She learned that John Brandeis had arrived in New York to join Stern Brothers nearly twenty-five years earlier, when his family-owned enterprise in the Midwest merged with the Manhattan retailer.

Omaha. Nebraska. She mouthed the words—so unfamiliar she wasn't even sure how to say them out loud. A place unknown to her, as foreign as the privileged lifestyle of this respected Jewish family. They were described as "community stewards" who established the first hospital open and free to all, helped to extend Omaha's park system, and developed programs for Russian immigrants. Their retailing giant in the Midwest was equal to Stern Brothers and was called "the biggest department store west of Chicago." At the 1907 opening of the Brandeis eight-story landmark skyscraper in downtown Omaha, "then eleven-year-old John Brandeis was accorded the honor of laying the cornerstone."

Zelda read how the Stern and Brandeis families became deeply connected—first through investments, then through marriage. In 1914, the businesses merged. The brothers-in-law, John Brandeis and Irving Stern, had worked side by side since John's father died.

She bent over the print to reread the next sentence, then sat back and released a sigh of relief. John's grandparents were Austrian Jewish immigrants.

∞∞

ON WEDNESDAY, ZELDA WOKE at dawn. Over the last several days, she and Giorgio had repeatedly practiced what she would say. Still, her stomach was in knots. In a matter of hours, she'd be face-to-face with John Brandeis. She had lied—at the very least *misled*—to get her way, surprising herself by her own daring. What was she becoming, resorting to deception like that? What if this all backfired? Taking in a deep breath and slowly releasing it, she summoned her purpose. This was about Lila and her family, she reminded herself. She would not be able to save the world, but she was determined to save these three souls.

Down the street from her building, she stopped at the small cafeteria where she always got a cup of coffee and the morning paper. She sat alone in a vinyl-covered booth, skimming bits of headlines, considering again her choice of words to a retail magnate of national prominence. In the dozen years since she left Vienna as an art curator, she'd never talked with a person of such high standing. She tried to remember that confident young woman, to call her back from what felt like a lifetime ago.

At the Waldorf that morning, Zelda worked with fierce focus. Each maid had to clean ten rooms and get approval from the manager on duty before taking her lunch break. Today of all days she was stuck with Stanislaw Polonsky, a taskmaster and stickler for details. She wore her treasured wristwatch that Giorgio had given her for her last birthday. She'd been surprised at the extravagance of the gift—she knew a Curvex cost thirty-five dollars, a luxury they couldn't afford. She normally didn't clean in it but did this morning because it kept her on task and, she thought, it was a nice touch, considering her meeting with Brandeis.

She glanced at the watch before removing it, then pulled on plastic gloves, which she did with each toilet cleaning. It was fifteen minutes after eleven. On her knees, she stooped over her tenth commode, scouring the insides with the latest product, Clorox bleach, until the white enamel shined. Pushing off from the floor, she stood up and turned to the sink, where she applied the same rigor.

By eleven thirty, with her quota of rooms done to Stanislaw's exacting standards, Zelda rode the elevator to the Waldorf basement office to clock out.

"Not so fast, Zelda." She jerked her head, startled by Stanislaw, who entered the room behind her. "Anna called in sick. We have to get her rooms cleaned before hotel check-in. I'm dividing them among the five of you. Take Rooms 711 and 712."

Zelda stood in disbelief. When she didn't move, he roared, "Get going! Now!"

She came close to walking out at that moment, losing her job and half their income. Instead she raced upstairs, cleaning furiously. It was past noon by the time she punched out. She scurried across the ornate Waldorf lobby past diners nestled in velvety banquettes in the Peacock Alley restaurant just as the two-ton bronze clock chimed, as it always did on the quarter hour. Pushing through the glass revolving doors, she dashed across Park Avenue heading west. *Just eight short blocks*, she told herself, turning south on Fifth.

Zelda battled her way around the crowds when she got to Stern Brothers. She hadn't counted on the mass of people lining up and pushing through the revolving doors. As she pressed forward to reach the elevator, the receptionist's warning, "not a minute late," rang its alarm. She tried to think of an explanation for her tardiness. Surely this had to be the store's busiest time, when local workers came to browse on their lunch hour. But that wouldn't explain her half an hour lapse.

As she entered the foyer outside Brandeis's office, she took a deep breath and smoothed her coat. The mahogany grandfather clock showed twenty-five minutes to one. She approached the receptionist's desk. "Hello. Remember me? Zelda Muni?" She tried to keep her voice steady. "I have an appointment with Mr. Brandeis."

The secretary looked up and frowned. "That appointment was for noon, Miss Muni. I'm afraid you've lost your chance."

Zelda's face tightened. "I . . . I had an emergency!"

"That's not Mr. Brandeis's problem. He's a busy man, and I instructed you to be punctual."

"I told you this was a matter of grave importance." Zelda's words were loud and demanding. "I am not leaving until I can see Mr. Brandeis."

She flopped onto the couch in the waiting room. That weasel Stanislaw. This heartless wench. Zelda tried to calm herself. She noticed a Stern Brothers brochure on the oval coffee table, its cover a picture of a smiling John Brandeis standing with Irving Stern. Next to it was the morning's *New York Times*. She picked up the paper, glared at its headline: "'Austria Is Now a State of the German Reich,' Hails Hitler."

This is not the Vienna we knew, Zelda. And time is running out.

The ringing of the full Westminster chime sequence startled her. When the reverberation ceased, the door to Brandeis's office opened, and a man of medium build in his early forties stepped out, a man she recognized. He wore a black suit, impeccably tailored. Zelda didn't see anyone else in the waiting room, so she rose quickly from the couch and stepped forward. "Mr. Brandeis, my name is Zelda Muni, and I must talk with you. It's extremely urgent." She tried to minimize her accent, precisely pronouncing each word.

He stared at her with a puzzled expression. The receptionist blurted, "She arrived late for your appointment, Mr. Brandeis. I told her to leave."

"Now, Mary, surely I have fifteen minutes to address—" He turned back to Zelda. "Is it Miss or Mrs. Muni?"

Zelda firmly shook the hand he extended to her, meeting his eyes as she answered. "It's Mrs., sir."

"As I said, Mary, I must have fifteen minutes available to address Mrs. Muni's concerns. Can you take her coat?"

"Actually, I'd prefer to keep it on, thank you." Zelda ran her hand across her hair before stepping into the wood-paneled office.

Mary nodded coldly to Zelda and closed the door behind them.

Brandeis walked to his stately Victorian desk and sat down. He motioned to the leather armchair facing him. "Give me just a moment."

She lowered herself into the chair, aware of the firmness of its tufted back. She watched him silently as he signed several documents, noticing the pearl pin in his royal blue tie, surely silk. She studied the spacious office. It was appointed in dark woods and softly illuminated by several Tiffany table lamps. Her eyes froze on an oil painting that felt familiar—its golden background and ornamental layout reminded her of Gustav Klimt, one of her favorite Viennese painters. When she turned back toward Brandeis, she saw he had been observing her and, blushing, she quickly looked down at her hands, rough and unseemly, holding them together on her lap, not knowing what else to do with them.

Brandeis moved his papers aside and leaned forward over his desk; his eyes seemed to take her in quickly and make an assessment. "So, what urgent matter has brought you here?"

She glanced at the mirror hanging on the wall behind him and caught her reflection, chestnut hair framing an oval face. Her uniform remained hidden; her immigrant status not yet firmly established. She caught the slight smell of cigar tobacco and cleared her throat before answering. "Mr. Brandeis, I have learned of your background and your success. I am also aware of your . . . your philosophy of responsibility to others."

It occurred to her he might think she was asking for something for herself, and she hastened to clarify. "I am not here on my own behalf. I left my native Austria in '26 with my Italian-born husband, hoping to do great things in this country. While our lives haven't turned out as we had planned, we are free and safe. That is not the case for my dearest childhood friend, her husband, and their teenage son. As Jews, they have run out of options."

Brandeis leaned back into his chair, his lips pursed. A pained look, like a shadow, crossed his face.

"I know you are a good man, a generous man. That you've always focused on giving the needy the opportunity to work. That you've used your good fortune for the welfare of many." She paused to steel herself for her next words. "I am here asking you, *begging* you, to consider three people—a husband and wife and their fifteen-year-old son. They need someone with credibility to vouch for them so they can obtain visas and immigrate as I have—as your ancestors have—to America."

She was aware of Brandeis's eyes on her. They were hazel with glints of green. Deep set, direct. His face had an intensity, a self-confidence, perhaps mixed with, what—sadness? She didn't know this man. Yet, in a way, she did. He was the boy, filled with pride, who laid the cornerstone for his family's new store; the one who watched his parents give back to people less fortunate. She bit her tongue, hoping her words had been persuasive.

Brandeis was still, off by himself someplace. It seemed he'd been holding his breath as he listened to her and just now let it out. "Mrs. Muni, you must care very deeply about this family to advocate for them." He paused as if collecting his thoughts. "I've received letters, many letters. Jews in New York and throughout the United States have also received such petitions from people who know people who need to leave Austria or Germany or Poland or Russia."

He turned his head, then spoke to the air. "And yet, naturally, I can't save everyone." His voice sounded weary. "From these letters, I can't even know whom to vouch for."

Of course Brandeis would have been asked to help others. There were throngs of Jews desperate to escape persecution, repression. Certainly, countless requests came from people he knew, not from some chambermaid. How foolish she was, how presumptuous. What was she thinking? Why did she imagine she could enlist him in the cause of Lila, Bart, and Eli, who were nothing more to him than faceless strangers?

The image of Lila and her family burst through Zelda's thoughts. A darkness was closing in on them. They were trapped. She wanted to shout, *They will die if you don't help them!*

His voice, sad and serious, brought her back. "Tell me more about these friends of yours, Mrs. Muni."

Brandeis's invitation hung in the air. Zelda at first felt immobilized by the weight of what she had to do. But, in his words, she heard a plea. And in Lila's as well.

You must help us reach America. You are our only hope, Zelda.

"Lila Rohm—that was her name before she married Bart Stoff. Lila lived close to my apartment building in Vienna's District Sixteen. We were both poor, relatively speaking, but with loving families. We were like sisters. I loved her like a sister." Zelda's eyes misted. She struggled to maintain her composure.

"We'd spend Sunday mornings in Stadtpark or attend an afternoon symphony. We'd exchange books we loved—Thomas Mann's *Death in Venice* or Kafka's *Metamorphosis*." Her mind raced as she grasped at the memories. "We shared a love for art and music. Lila played the piano—Mozart, Schubert, and Haydn were her favorites. We grew up at a time when a Catholic and a Jew could live and study and work side by side. Today—"

"Mrs. Muni, you are not Jewish?" Brandeis interrupted. He stared in astonishment. "I suppose I should have known that from your name."

"I am Catholic, as is my husband. We met during a skiing holiday near the Austrian-Italian border. Giorgio was studying structural engineering not far from his hometown. I was studying art history at the University of Vienna. His dream was to come to the United States to design and build bridges. When he graduated, I was already working as an art curator. We got married and were among the fortunate to obtain visas and . . ." Zelda stopped, her cheeks burning.

"Go on, Mrs. Muni." Brandeis's face relaxed, and Zelda caught a flicker of warmth in his eyes. "While some gentiles seek to help the Jews, you are the first who has come to me."

She straightened in her chair. "Because of Hitler's strict racial policies, I couldn't even associate with the Stoffs if I still lived in Austria." Brandeis nodded, suddenly pensive.

"Lila is a teacher but can no longer work in the public schools. Her kind husband owned a small uniform manufacturing company that has been seized. Their teenage son, Eli, is spat on, bullied, and humiliated on the very street where he lives. They have no option but to escape while that's even still possible."

"And you have reached out to me." He inched forward, his expression just then like someone in torment.

She'd never considered the awesome responsibility of someone like Brandeis, a wealthy American Jew, his entire culture and people being threatened from afar. In a way, they were all trapped. Lila by the Nazis. Zelda by her lowly status, powerless to save her friends, except through this desperate gamble. And Brandeis by his guilt, his sense of futility at the vastness of the danger and how few he could rescue.

"You can do this," she submitted. At that moment, Zelda realized she was giving him permission to act. "If I may be blunt, sir, you have that power. I am just an immigrant chambermaid."

Brandeis remained silent. Zelda became aware of the ticking of a clock; for a second, she broke his gaze and turned toward the sound. She could hear her heart beating and swallowed hard, knowing she had done what she set out to do. There was nothing more she could say to him.

Finally, his mouth stretched ever so slightly into a smile. "But you, Mrs. Muni, you have more power than you think." He stood, walked out from behind his desk, and grasped her hand in his.

A BRILLIANT SUN MET Zelda as she left the department store. It was as though spring had burst forth without warning. She felt a light breeze glance across her face and stood for a moment to relish it before she retraced her steps along the crowded sidewalks. She thought about what she might pick up at the grocery on her way home from work. Perhaps some crisp lettuce and red peppers, garlic and olive oil for a fresh salad. She'd stop at the butcher and get pounded veal. Yes, some *Wiener Schnitzel* like her mother used to make would be perfect. Giorgio would like that very much.

And, after dinner, she would write back to Lila.

THE SUITCASE

August 1938

"THERE WILL ONLY BE three affidavits!" Lila cried out loud to no one in particular. Her letter to Zelda told of Bart losing his small company, of Eli being bullied. In her harried state, she hadn't thought to share that her mother, now in poor health, lived with them. That Mutti, too, needed a way out of Austria.

"I will write her back, tell her—"

"There's no time for that, Lila." Jenny leaned forward from her wooden wheelchair. She squeezed Lila's hand. "I couldn't handle the trip to America. And I won't leave your father."

Lila realized the truth in her mother's words, but it was no easier to accept. After her beloved Vati died last year, they lay him to rest in the Jewish section of Vienna's *Zentralfriedhof*. Her mother had visited the cemetery often when she was steadier on her feet. Now that the gravesite visits were rare, Jenny seemed to equate leaving Vienna with abandoning her husband's memory.

Zelda's letter should have been cause for celebration. She'd found a New York businessman to vouch for the three of them so they could go to America. To live in a country that allowed belief without restraint. Where citizenship meant that people have the right to choose their own destinies, where each can speak and think freely.

But at what cost?

"I could ask Zelda to talk to this man. He sounds generous and kind. He'd certainly agree." Even as she said this, Lila doubted she could undo a complicated sponsorship process likely in motion well before the letter from Zelda arrived.

"These Germans won't bother old ladies like me. I'll be fine. I can move in with Aunt Miriam."

∞∞∞

LILA STIRRED. HER EYES fluttered, and her mouth twitched. She caught a slight movement in the loosely woven voile of curtains, recalling the window she'd left open the previous evening. She fixated on the ineffectual breeze. It was, again, too early to be up, the summer heat compounding her fitfulness. Fully awake now, she heard her quickened heartbeats pounding in her ears. So much to consider and so little time.

"Why can't I take my skis?" Eli had pleaded with her yesterday, until she told him they were only permitted two suitcases.

"And one suitcase will be for all the things that will help us remember." Lila had wrung her hands as she spoke, her eyes surely taking on a crazed look that she knew scared her son. "Other things we can get in America."

A month had passed since Zelda's letter arrived, exuding excitement that she had a guarantor for their passage. This is what Lila wanted. What she had hoped for. But now the reality was closing in on her. They were to leave their home. Not just their home but their country, their life as they knew it. And they were leaving Mutti, though Lila saw this as only temporary.

She planned to send for her mother after they were settled. But how? And how would Mutti get along without her? Since Vati's death, being there for Mutti had become Lila's purpose.

There was so much unknown.

Lila tried to push away those debilitating thoughts. She had to focus on the packing and transporting of physical objects. What to take, what to leave behind? She envied her husband and son, their lack of wistfulness or sentimentality. Bart suggested she gather practical items to ease their transition. Eli wanted to bring his most treasured possessions, like the skis or his jazz albums.

But, for Lila, the tangible embodiment of her family— her culture, her memories—had to fit into her suitcase. Her favorite piano compositions by Haydn, Mozart, Schubert, and Schoenberg. Some of the watercolors she'd sketched during quiet Sundays in Stadtpark, far from their poor, urban neighborhood. The family photo album—those early prints of Mutti and Vati, of Aunt Miriam, along with her other aunts and uncles and cousins, now mostly dispersed, and of her adored first cousin Arthur. A recent formal portrait of her with Eli and Bart. The box of letters she kept. And her beloved books, although she knew she could only carry a few favorites—one from each: Franz Kafka, Joseph Roth, Stefan Zweig.

Her mother had offered the most basic advice: "Take a blanket and pillow, for God's sake!" Their small group of friends in their predominantly non-Jewish neighborhood suggested transporting food that might keep or, as Max Rothstein advised, "Bring anything that can be exchanged for American dollars."

Lila rose soundlessly so as not to disturb Bart, slipped on her robe, and slowly walked through their cluttered two-bedroom flat. She eyed every shelf, every photograph, every souvenir they'd ever bought or received. A dull ache above her eyes spread to the top of her head as she asked herself over and over: *What do I put in this suitcase? What do I want to carry along with me?*

∞∞∞

STANDING BEHIND THEIR TIGHTLY packed belongings in the seaport town of Trieste, bracing herself for a long journey, Lila couldn't shake the churning in her gut. She kept telling herself she was getting out, after all, with Bart and Eli. But her mind fixed on the others. What would happen to the Rothsteins? And Bella, her colleague at the school that fired the two of them with no explanation? *And Mutti, my dearest Mutti. Will I ever see you again? There is a trail I am leaving behind*, she thought, *and soon it will simply disappear.*

She eased herself down onto one of their suitcases and took a handkerchief out of her pocket to wipe the back of her neck. Slipping off her shoes, she felt the damp grain as she curled her toes into the sand. A cacophony of conversations carried over the sound of wind and gulls and waves lapping toward shore. Mostly Italian, but also German, Czech, and Hungarian. Inhaling the salty air, she scanned the expanse of a now-hidden beach, blanketed by the hundreds of families who had also planted themselves and their belongings along this coastline in northeastern Italy. All awaiting the ship that would take them into the Adriatic Sea and then across to America.

She looked over at Eli, soothed by the hopefulness in his stance. She watched him approach another boy about his age. They found a ball and began to kick it back and forth across the sand. One shot bounced off a man's back. He turned and smiled at the boys. Eli waved back, and she saw that twinkle in his eye that always won him friends. This is what she needed to focus on today. Her Eli. He was outgoing, confident, resilient. In America, he could have a promising future. After all, when he was only ten, he had been chosen for *Realgymnasium*, a program devoted to modern languages and science studies for the most capable.

She counted backward. That was the year Hitler became Germany's chancellor, the year the turmoil seeped into Austria. She hadn't noticed at first, so immersed was she in Eli, the family, her job. German refugees trickled into Vienna. Bella was one of them, and as the women grew closer at work, Bella shared stories about the building of prisons and the laws enacted to deprive Jews of their rights as workers and citizens. Some hoped for things to improve in Austria. Lila envisioned a more frightening vista. She had pressed Bart about finding a safer haven while they still could and had reached out to her old friend Zelda Muni. By the time the sponsorships came through in late August, the Stoffs had new passport IDs stamped with a *J*.

The sound of a sharp whistle pulled Lila out of her reverie. She looked up to see a large ocean liner approaching the harbor, its towering apparition otherworldly.

"It's here! Where's Papa?" Eli, his only white collared shirt now drenched in sweat, lifted the other suitcase and rushed toward the queue forming at the dock.

Lila called after him that she'd be close behind. With each step she took toward the ship, it grew taller, forcing her to tip her head fully back to follow the curved bow. She turned to scan for Bart among the crowd and spotted him farther down the beach with a man she recognized from their neighborhood. She followed Bart's gaze to the advancing vessel, its dark hull forming a sharp point that sliced through the emerald sea like a blade. She shouted his name several times, waving to get his attention. So many thoughts swirled inside her head as she watched him bound, grinning, across the sand. Bart always had an easier time being happy, one of the reasons their pairing worked for her. She brooded. His thoughts were simple;

nothing kept him awake at night. She was a pessimist, he an optimist. At times, she felt him incapable of deep inquiry and considered him beneath her intellectually. Now, she was grateful to have his buoyant spirit to counter her inner turbulence.

∞∞

THE TRIP ACROSS THE Atlantic lasted nearly two weeks. As they careened toward America, the division of passengers was conspicuous: the affluent comfortably ensconced in staterooms and cabins; the rest of them crammed in tight quarters below. After a while, it didn't matter how tasteless the American food was. More than once, Lila thought she would die from the nausea. The sickly stench reeked throughout the steerage, the sound of retching only fueling her queasiness.

Now, the ship's foghorn sounded three deep blasts. Lila had been trying to rest—they all had as the rhythm of the sea calmed beneath them—when the piercing noise brought her to her feet. She could feel the waves shift course and sensed the boat slowing. She pulled a sweater over her blouse, shoved on her shoes, and shook Bart's shoulder, then Eli's. "Hurry! Land must be near!"

They ran up to the deck as the engines throttled back. Commotion erupted. Yelling and screaming drew Lila, Eli, and Bart toward the bow. Strangers hugged one another, weeping with joy. Eli grabbed her arm and pulled them forward until they could steady against the rails. Water splashed against the hull, exploding into sparkling arcs. A cool breeze bathed her face. Squeezing Eli's hand on her left and Bart's on her right, Lila searched the harbor, then spotted the enormous beacon of liberty rising from the sea: a stone sculpture of a robed female bearing a torch aloft. Lila drank in the rush of salty air, tipsy as it filled her lungs, immobilized as if in a stupor. This grand lady with her right arm held high seemed to welcome all of them to America. Lila glanced at Eli. His eyes were gleaming, his smile jubilant.

A voice boomed across the deck. "Gather your belongings. A ferry will deliver you to port!"

Lila raced to the bottom level with Eli and Bart at her heels as she tried to organize her thoughts, scattered wildly, as were all the personal effects in their quarters, apparently displaced when the boat shifted and turned toward land. Amid the disarray, she began grabbing stray items, cramming them into her open suitcase. Her head spinning, she scrutinized their small space. Where was the framed photo of Mutti? Lila silently gasped, a lump caught in her throat.

Just behind her, Eli stepped to the side onto the blanket, partially lying on the floor. A soft snap sounded as he put his foot down then retracted it, almost losing his balance. He pulled the coverlet back on the bed and bent down to retrieve the framed picture, pausing, bringing it to his lips, unaware of his mother's eyes on him. The glass was cracked, the photo unharmed. Eli sheepishly turned to hand her the damaged mounting.

"It's fine. All that matters is the photograph." She felt it solid in her hands but knew what remained was paper-thin and would yellow over time. She placed the broken frame between two sweaters and secured the leather suitcase.

Bart touched her arm. "*Bereit zu gehen?*"

Lila drew in a breath and slowly exhaled to calm her nerves. "Yes, ready."

Bart took the heavier bag, Eli seized the other, and they joined the queue moving up the metal stairs. Hundreds upon hundreds of immigrants filled the deck, packed together, luggage in hand, misshapen duffels slung over their shoulders, a derby or scarf catching in a gust of wind.

"Mama, you need to push forward." At Eli's prompting, Lila quickened her pace. Bart motioned the two to get in front of him as they exited the steamship onto the ferryboat.

∞∞∞

OFFICERS WEARING UNIFORMS GREETED each person as the transport moored at Ellis Island. One man shouted out instructions to walk down the gangplank to the main building. He handed Lila a numbered tag. She understood him perfectly but saw from her husband's puzzled expression that he hadn't. Like Bart, many understood little English. A discordance of languages erupted into mayhem until a column began to form. The men helped women and children struggling with their trunks, cloth sacks, and suitcases as they disembarked, following one another along a path. Soon they all entered an imposing red brick structure.

With identity badges affixed to their outerwear, Lila, Bart, and Eli stepped into a large ground-floor room. They were told to leave their belongings there, that they would undergo a review process. Explanations got repeated in English, German, and Italian. In a wave of panic, Lila addressed the American official in German, asking if the suitcases would be safe. She repeated her question, more calmly, in English.

He nodded. "Absolutely." As if responding to the apprehension in her eyes, he added, "You needn't worry."

Fingers pointed up a winding staircase; the sound of footsteps surrounded her as she led the ascent to the registry room for medical and legal evaluations. The waiting area had long metal rails that seemed to facilitate an orderly procession. Several older immigrants left the queue to rest on wooden benches.

Her jaw dropped as she entered the grand hall. She'd never seen an indoor space this enormous. The noise of thousands of voices bounced off the vaulted ceilings.

Compared to their time sitting and waiting, the medical exam took but seconds—a rapid head-to-toe scan. Lila was told to continue through the maze of metal rails toward the far end of the chamber for her legal inspection. When she finally heard her name called, she marched forward and found herself face-to-face with a uniformed inspector seated on a stool behind a high desk.

"Where were you born?"

"Vienna."

"Are you married?"

Lila turned and pointed to Bart and Eli. "There. My husband sits with our son."

The officer motioned for the two to join her, and he paused before he addressed all of them. "What is your occupation, Mr. Stoff?"

Lila hesitated, not used to speaking for her husband. "My husband had a small business and will be looking for work. I teach English. Our son is a . . . He will be enrolled in school."

"Have any of you ever been convicted of a crime?"

"No."

"How much money do you have?"

"I . . . I don't know. Very little."

"What is your destination?"

"New York City." Lila paused, then added, "For now."

He stamped papers and handed them to her. "Walk down the left aisle." He pointed to the stairs and then called out the next name.

She took off briskly, almost gleeful to have this interrogation behind them. At the top of the stairs, she scanned the first floor of the building. There was a post office, a ticketing booth for the railways, and a separate room to change money. Blackboards posted the exchange rate for a variety of currencies. She noticed several people holding up signs. She had been instructed to connect with the Hebrew Immigrant Aid Society. A social worker would meet them and, she had been assured, have the keys to their living quarters. HIAS would cover the cost of the apartment along with modest living expenses for the next three months as they decided their future.

Whoops and yelps of joy broke through her absorption. The ground floor had turned into some kind of meeting place where family and friends connected with loved ones. As she scoured the scene, her alarm returned. She couldn't see the suitcases. They weren't where she'd placed them when they arrived. Lila's eyes darted from one area to another until she spotted a great mountain of luggage sectioned off with tape. Heaving a sigh of relief, she felt Bart's arm on her shoulder. Bart and Eli nudged her along, and as they picked their way down the stairs, she grew lightheaded. The long journey was finally over.

"Lila!"

When she heard her name, Lila twisted her head toward the familiar voice. She recognized Zelda instantly, her chestnut hair now in a bun, her oval face thinner but beaming with a broad grin. She took in Giorgio's black curls, her eyes filling before she nearly tripped over luggage in her path. The Munis swooped her up into their arms.

"My God!" Lila tried to speak through her sobs. "Twelve years and we're finally together." She pulled away to take in first Zelda then Giorgio before she clasped them again. "Our angels."

Bart and Eli stood awkwardly several steps behind Lila. She turned and grabbed Eli's arm and pulled him forward. "You remember my Eli? He was three when you left for America."

Zelda's eyes teared as she reached up to kiss Eli's cheek. Giorgio wrapped his arms around Lila and Eli at once. Bart stepped forward murmuring, "*Danke, danke, danke,*" as he took Giorgio's outstretched hand and gave Zelda a squeeze. For several blissful moments, the five were entangled.

"But I am not your sponsor, dear Bart," Zelda murmured. "I was merely the small vessel who found the large ship."

Eli looked puzzled. "What do you mean?"

"Zelda's referring to the man . . . an important New York businessman. She actually got him to vouch for us, to sign for our affidavits." Lila held her son's gaze, realizing that in the anxious scurry of those last days in Vienna, with Eli preoccupied himself, she had not thought or found the time to speak about the American businessman. "This John Brandeis, he's our angel as well."

"But why—"

"Excuse me, excuse me. Are you the Stoffs?" Lila turned her head, this time toward an unfamiliar voice, bewildered at being fingered amid this boisterous throng. She found herself facing a blue sign with large bold letters in white: HIAS. She squinted to read the words in smaller print: "Welcome The Refugee."

∞∞

THE SCENE AS THEY exited the inspection hall kept flashing through Lila's mind, though it was now a full month ago. Lucy Shorr, the HIAS representative, had transported the three and their belongings to where they now temporarily resided: a low-rise tenement on Orchard Street, just a dozen blocks from Zelda and Giorgio's apartment.

With its brick face and fire escape, their building looked like every other lining this street. Here they lived among other immigrants, surrounded by bargain shops, lingerie stores, bars, Jewish-owned haberdasheries, and the smells from kosher and Chinese restaurants. Signs with Hebrew lettering filled the windows. The nearby Laundromat promoted cleaned suits for a dollar. The tailor offered pressing along with repairs. Sidewalk peddlers, cigarettes hanging out of their mouths, held out bags of fresh cauliflower, celery stalks, and zucchini for pass-ersby. Bedsheets hung from iron balconies. Street workers sat on curbs, fanning themselves with their caps. Women covered themselves in dark shawls despite the heat. For some Eastern Europeans coming from shtetls, Lila understood how the Lower East Side could feel comforting with its familiar, old-world flavor. But she came from a city of operas and waltzes, art galleries and stunning architecture. She reminded herself these were provisional accommodations, and they were safe here.

She'd tried to make the stark apartment into a home for them, placing her watercolors on the walls, displaying the family pictures and collection of books. She positioned the frame holding her mother's image prominently on the single credenza in the living room, the crack now reaching diagonally from top to bottom.

Today, Bart planned to meet with a HIAS specialist about job prospects. Lila pressed him not to make any commitments. She had been willing to give New York a try and crammed their days with activities, despite her reservations about making the city their permanent home. She and Bart had met friends of the Munis and had several dinners together, but Lila didn't feel they fit in. They'd spent their first weekend on Coney Island on a beach packed with bathers as far as the eye could see. The southern shore of Long Island reminded her of the chaotic beach scene in Trieste, except here she had faced a sea of scant swimsuits donned by women who appeared insouciant while she felt self-conscious. Weeks later, the three attended a Brook-lyn Dodgers game at Ebbets Field. Eli pointed out the patches worn by the players, promoting the 1939 World's Fair to be held in New York. Lacking an understanding of baseball and disconnected from the shouts and cheers, all Lila had noticed was a mass of mostly men's heads, their straw boaters and derbies clouding the bleachers.

Then, last Sunday, they'd caught an early train from Grand Central to visit Bart's first cousin in New Rochelle. The station swarmed with people, the din of their voices disorienting as it competed with the sounds of pigeons flapping against the arched ceiling. Sunlight flooded through windows in the vaulted main room of the terminal, illuminating the central concourse and its long row of ticket booths. A kind man at the information kiosk guided them to the right window, then to the stairs that led to the platforms. When the ride along the north shore of Long Island Sound took them past the Bronx, Eli enthusiastically identified Yankee Stadium and the zoo. Lila took pleasure in his exuberance yet wished she could be more hopeful about what lay in front of them. As they moved farther from the city, the landscape opened up and grew greener and she finally loosened up, happy to escape the hustle of the urban ghetto. But despite the comfort of being amongst relatives, she'd felt even more displaced in Westchester County, missing her own family.

So now, Lila gave Bart a quick kiss and reminded him he was only exploring job possibilities in the unlikely event they stayed. They still had two months to decide, two months before they needed to position themselves to be self-sufficient. She felt cheerful this early fall morning as she left their apartment with Eli, the air crisp, a cerulean sky above. The two passed a teeming marketplace of peddlers, their side-by-side pushcarts filled with vegetables, fruits, chickens, and breads lining the curbs on the way to the Delancey and Essex Streets subway.

Today Eli was taking her on a tour of Midtown Manhattan. He had insisted. Times Square was their first destination. "It's the heart of the world," Eli said with some authority. As they threaded their way through the crowds, bold billboards caught Lila's attention. *THE NEW CHEVROLET 1938: The Car That Is Complete* ran next to ads for Bromo-Seltzer and Calvert Whiskies. The Times Building, Loew's State Theatre, Hotel Astor, and Gaiety

Theatre were conspicuous across the wide street. A garish poster promoted a live burlesque show with the image of scantily dressed women in a dance line. Here, too, Lila had a bad taste in her mouth. How crass it all was—nothing like her beloved Vienna.

Suddenly a passerby jostled her without a word of apology. Eli prodded her forward, and they zigzagged from one street to another. Lila observed the wider avenues and sidewalks and the taller buildings in limestone as they walked eastward. Eli noted the near-complete construction of a skyscraper complex being built by a wealthy businessman named Rockefeller. She was impressed with her son's grasp of facts and ease navigating the urban jumble and told him so.

"Mama, I wonder. Does this John Brandeis work somewhere around here?"

Eli's question caught Lila by surprise. "I—I don't know." She hadn't considered this man as an actual person they could seek out and didn't know if that was even appropriate. "Sometimes, people do noble acts without expecting . . . without wanting anything in return. We are the beneficiaries of this man's good will and generosity of spirit."

"So, we can't find out where he works and go thank him?"

"Not now, Eli. We can think about how we might express our appreciation someday, okay?"

They walked ahead silently for a few blocks. As they passed Radio City Music Hall, Eli resumed his descriptive hyperbole. "This is the largest theater in the world!" Lila wasn't sure if this was her son's interpretation or a description from the New York City pocket guide he carried along with him: "'From these modern skyscrapers, you can see all of New York!'" he read. Lila was more interested in following her nose to the aroma of roasted chestnuts.

By noon, they stood at the foot of the Chrysler Building at the corner of Forty-Second and Lexington, its metallic sheen and art deco style gaining Lila's full scrutiny. The day remained cloudless and she craned her neck, squinting to admire the silver spire flashing in the sun. She didn't care that this elegant edifice "used to be the world's tallest building," another fact Eli drew from his guide. He took the elevator to the Chrysler observation deck on the seventy-first floor, as she stood amid mostly men hovering around cars that filled the lobby, smoothing their hands along the elongated shiny black metal hoods, pointing to the whitewall tires. Lila thought it strange to see automobiles inside a building. She gawked at the admiring crowd, barely noticing Eli walking toward her.

Uneasy with the heights of New York skyscrapers, Lila also remained at ground level at their next and final stop: the Empire State Building. Eli set off to climb the 102 stories to the top. A rite of passage, he'd called it. Seeking fresh air, she pushed through the brass door and waited for a streetcar to pass before crossing for another view of the landmark building.

Men's voices caught her attention, and she stole a sidelong glance at two workers sitting along a ledge of a building under construction, eating sandwiches on what must have been their lunch break.

"You ever listen to that priest on the radio?"

"That Coughlin guy?"

"Yeah, I been hearing his broadcasts every week."

A small boy ran past Lila, his mother shouting after him, blocking the conversation Lila hadn't meant to listen in on. She gingerly stepped closer to the men.

"He says those Jew bankers caused the Depression. Some international conspiracy."

"He said that?"

"Somethin' like that. There's a lot more of 'em around this city, that's for sure. 'specially downtown. Pretty pushy folk, if you ask me."

"Yeah, lots of foreigners. I'd like to send them Jews back where they came from."

Lila stood frozen, her back to the men so they couldn't see the anger surely coloring her face and neck. She felt like she had the first time Eli was attacked on his way home from school: when she went to greet him and saw his clothes torn, a bruise on his forehead. He had been kicked and verbally taunted right in their neighborhood. She wanted to harm these men, just like she'd wanted to find Eli's tormentors and slap them senseless, but instead she darted across the street. Blinded by her fury, she ran in the path of an oncoming car. It screeched to a stop, honking at her as she fled back into the Empire State Building.

Eli was just exiting the elevator. "Mama, you look like you saw a ghost." His face darkened, and he put his hands on her shoulders. "Are you all right?"

Lila shook her head as if expelling a swarm of gnats from her hair. "I'm fine. I crossed the street and got in the way of a car. Just wasn't paying attention."

∞∞∞

"THERE ARE MORE IMMIGRANTS pouring into New York by the hour," Lila said as she set a bowl of vegetables and a pitcher of water on the worn oak table for dinner. She couldn't hide her fretfulness. It was nearly October, darkness already setting in at six o'clock. But their small apartment was always under-lit, having only two windows, one in the bedroom above the sewing machine Lila got on sale and used to earn extra spending money. The other window, here in the dining room, faced another building.

"*Du bist* . . . again, how you say . . . *ruhig*?" In the short time they'd been in New York, Bart's comprehension had improved, and he picked up new words in English every day.

Lila insisted they were in America and should speak the language of their new country.

"Restless. Yes. I am restless." Her diction was perfect. After all, English was what she taught before she was summarily dismissed from her school as anti-Semitism began infusing the country.

"We've been *hier—was? Zwei* months?" Bart ran his hand over his bald scalp.

"I don't see opportunities here, Bart. Not for you, and certainly not for Eli." Lila spooned several clumps of mashed potatoes onto Eli's plate. "I contacted HIAS and asked them about smaller cities where there's a university. Somewhere we can assimilate." Unspoken was her hope that people outside of New York would be more accepting. That they could live in a neighborhood with real homes, with trees in the backyards like she'd seen in New Rochelle. Where Eli could get a college education.

Bart reached for the platter of brisket, a luxury she allowed sparingly on their stipend, although she really wanted to splurge on veal for *Wiener Schnitzel*. He paused to gaze across the table at Lila. "Ah. *Du hast* been busy. *Was . . .* what . . . you *finden?*"

"They gave me a list of cities in the Midwest—St. Louis, Chicago, Columbus. I think Chicago is too big."

"I vote for Columbus." Eli put down his fork and wiped his mouth with his napkin. "Remember that Negro man, Jesse Owens? He's the one who showed Hitler that the Aryans aren't always the best. During the '36 Olympics—"

"I'm not sure what you're getting at, Eli." Lila made a mental note to bring out her homemade Viennese butter cookies.

"He was a student at Ohio State University. That's in Columbus."

Lila and Bart exchanged glances. She saw a twinkle of pride in Bart's eyes and could barely hold back a grin. "Well, *der Sohn*, I guess we need to find out a little more about Columbus, Ohio, then."

IN LESS THAN TWO weeks, arrangements were finalized for their move. After a day of last-minute errands ending with a makeshift dinner of leftovers, Lila gathered some newspapers, eased herself into the living room armchair, and clicked on the floor lamp. She opened the *New York Times* and was drawn to an article about FDR's static immigration policy, unraveling her thread of hope of getting her mother out of Vienna. She glanced over at the worn credenza, now covered with an embroidery she'd sewn, her eyes settling on Mutti's face, gazing out at her from behind the fractured glass.

It was in '26 that Lila had taken this portrait with her new Leica. She'd spent the savings from her teaching job on a camera to record Eli's childhood. She remembered the exact day—March 9—because it fell on Eli's third birthday and she thought it good practice to first shoot subjects who might sit still. The sparkle in Mutti's eyes and her winsome smile were for Eli and Vati, playing outside the frame of the picture. The day was unseasonably warm and sunny, still winter but pleasant enough to enjoy a walk—really a chase—in Stadtpark. Austria's economy had stabilized. The Great Depression hadn't yet arrived. Her life was happy: Bart's small business was growing, Eli was a daily delight, her parents were healthy. Studying the photograph now, she saw how well she'd captured Mutti's essence—her hair salt-and-pepper at sixty-five, her expression tender, the tilt in her chin exuding a grace and confidence.

Much as she physically resembled her mother, Lila yearned to possess her same plucky nature. She sat rigidly, a stream of random worries filling her head. What would it be like in Columbus, a town to which they had no connection? Who were these people, the Goldsteins, that HIAS said would take them into their home until they were able to get on their feet? Lila always found herself dwelling on the uncertainties that fed her anxiety before she considered more pleasant scenarios.

She had seen some pictures of Columbus. Sketches, really, by a cartoonist named James Thurber in back issues of *The New Yorker*. She learned that he was born there and attended Ohio State, so she bought a used copy of his autobiography, *My Life and Hard Times*, at a nearby bookshop. She adored his recollections of the chaos and frustrations of family and boyhood growing up, and the authentic human nature conveyed in its pages.

With Bart and Eli cleaning up dinner, she walked to Eli's closet-like room and stood amid his souvenirs. The Yankees cap. The cherished pennant from last week's World Series win over the Chicago Cubs at Yankee Stadium. The program from Benny Goodman's January Carnegie Hall jazz concert that Eli found in a pile of leftovers on Fifty-Seventh Street. Several new Count Basie albums. A photo of Joe Louis after his June win over Nazi favorite Max Schmeling for the world heavyweight boxing championship. Lila couldn't help but smile at Eli's American enthusiasms. She knew he would be fine wherever they settled.

Suddenly a longing for the country she once knew washed over her. Mutti and Vati. Aunt Miriam and the Rothsteins. Bella and her students. Quiet Sundays in Stadtpark. Her eyes filled. The undertow of the past wouldn't let go of its pull on her.

Tomorrow she'd haul out their two suitcases and pack everything she'd brought from Vienna. Eli had recently bought a small bag to carry all his new memorabilia. Bart approached their move philosophically—what will be will be, he said. She couldn't argue with that. Whatever came, it would be a new chapter.

WHEN THE LIGHTS DIMMED

1938–1939

HERSHEL WOULD NEVER FORGET the November day the Stoffs came to live with his family. They had an old-world look, like pictures he saw in his history books. Mr. and Mrs. Stoff dressed like Hershel's own Russian grandparents, each carrying a single suitcase—worn tweed with stripes and wooden handles. The mother had an accent, and the father didn't even speak English yet. The boy—Eli—looked to be Hershel's age, fifteen, with coffee-dark eyes that twinkled when he smiled. And Eli smiled a lot. Hershel instantly liked him.

For weeks, Hershel's parents had been briefing him and his brother about their temporary guests. How they'd had to leave their home in Vienna; how as Jews they had been taunted and threatened. Hershel couldn't imagine things bad enough to force his family to leave their house on the east side of Columbus. Sure, some months back he'd heard Jimmy Bragard call Max Sherman a "kike." But Mrs. Grason had grabbed Jimmy by the ear and set him down on a stool next to her desk for the rest of the period, then had him write an apology to Max and his family. Stuff like that just wasn't tolerated at Central High. Still, some things were accepted. Like the housing restrictions keeping Jews from moving to any neighborhood. It explained why Hershel's family lived in their Jewish enclave. But they were comfortable there. Hershel always felt safe.

So, nothing had braced him for the panic that erupted all through his neighborhood the same day the Stoffs arrived, as news spread about the looting and destruction of Jewish homes, hospitals, schools, shops, and synagogues in Germany and Austria. They'd called it *Kristallnacht*—"Night of Broken Glass"—because of the shards that littered the streets from all the smashed windows. The emerging pictures of Jews being beaten, furniture and goods being flung out of houses and stores, frightened them. It immediately bonded his family and the Stoffs, the seven of them huddling around the radio listening to the drama unfolding. Hershel's father said it reminded him of the pogroms in Imperial Russia in the late 1880s. Mrs. Stoff got especially hysterical when she heard that all of Vienna's twenty-one synagogues were attacked, the fires and bombs mostly destroying them. Through her sobs, she shared that several were located near their home district and fretted about her mother, who was still living there. Mr. Stoff kept repeating "*Mein Gott*," his arm wrapped tightly around his wife as they all sat in shock. It was one of the few times Eli wasn't smiling, his expression somber as he stood behind his parents, his hands on their shoulders.

Emma and Simon Goldstein were first-generation Americans, so Hershel never heard anything but English at home, except for the occasional Yiddish expression—*oy vey, chutzpah, klutz, kvell*—thrown in for embellishment. They'd met in Cleveland, where all of his grandparents had settled at the turn of the century. His mother's family came from Latvia, Papa's from Russia. After his parents married in 1922, they moved to Columbus so his father could join Uncle Jacob in his kosher meat business in the Jewish section of town, the east end. Hershel was born the next year, Meyer five years later. Soon, more immigrants arrived needing work, the Depression hit, and times became hard for everyone. Hershel was too young to be aware of any of that, but he clearly remembered when his mother opened a shop just a block from their house, on 571 Rich Street. It became a hub for the neighborhood, where the refugee women's baking and sewing skills could earn them a small income. He knew because he practically grew up there.

Living in such close quarters, Hershel saw how hard those early weeks were for the Stoffs, and mostly for Eli's mother. Because of her command of English—she'd been an English teacher in Vienna—she was the one reaching out to landlords to find them a place of their own. She kept telling Hershel's mother she didn't want to be a burden. The discrimination toward foreigners and especially Jewish immigrants like Lila— doors literally slammed in her face—alongside the horrors in Europe, wore on her. They wore on the household. But after their tumultuous arrival, the Stoffs began to feel part of the community. Mrs. Stoff joined the cadre of bakers at 571 and got to know many of the women in the neighborhood. Mr. Stoff got a job as a stockman at a uniform company where his broken English almost fit in. On Sundays, Hershel's parents played canasta with Eli's. And he and Eli, sometimes with Meyer in tow, spent much of their free time together.

∞∞∞

THE BOYS WALKED THE four blocks to Broad Street the morning winter break ended, Eli's first day at an American school. It had been snowing for an hour, the first snowfall since the Stoffs arrived with their suitcases two months earlier. They were the kind of large individual flakes that drifted slowly to the ground and stuck, producing a film of white wherever they landed. Hershel's winter field jacket and Eli's wool overcoat, along with the book bags slung over their shoulders, took on a glistening sheen. With the road fully blanketed, several Monday-morning drivers honked their impatience.

Eli took advantage of the slowed traffic and crossed the street, Hershel right behind him. "I see a bus coming up now!" Eli blurted out.

Once inside, Hershel dropped two coins for them in the box and walked down the aisle, losing his balance as the bus lurched forward. He motioned to Eli, and they slid into the first two open seats.

"I'm not ready to get back to school." Hershel slouched in the vinyl seat. "And to make it worse, they put you in the senior class. Are you nervous? I mean, all this will be new for you."

Even though he wouldn't turn sixteen for two months, Eli had tested into the upper grade. "More excited than nervous. But I'm not happy about being a senior. We could've been in all the same classes."

It was what Hershel liked about Eli. Sharing his disappointment and not gloating that he seemed to have a pretty big brain in that head of his.

They got off the bus and walked across South Washington Boulevard to Central High's entrance. "Pretty nice, eh? How does it compare to your school in Vienna?"

Eli scanned the building and grounds before he answered. "It reminds me of the Musikverein—our most famous concert hall. It's in the Innere Stadt. That's Vienna's Old Town."

Hershel nodded, somewhat surprised a friend of his would know about concert halls. "Did you go to performances there?"

"We did. The famous classical composers were born or lived in Vienna. Music was part of the air we breathed." Eli pointed toward the south wing of the U-shaped building. "Central High extends toward your Scioto River. The Musikverein was quite near the Wien. Both buildings are neoclassical. So they're similar—in design and location."

"Well, maybe at school you want to talk more about Ohio State football than concert halls and classical music." Hershel punched Eli playfully. "If you want to make any friends, you know?"

∞∞∞

"I GOT A PART-TIME job at the junkyard where they keep all those old cars and car parts," Eli announced.

"What're they paying you?" Hershel worked over at The Main Street Theatre for fifteen cents an hour. A good deal, he thought, since he loved movies and could watch the same film a dozen times in a week if he liked it.

"Twenty cents an hour."

The boys were sitting in the Goldsteins' kitchen on a cold day in February watching Eli's mother pound veal into a paper-thin sheet. *Wiener Schnitzel* was fast becoming Hershel's favorite dish, and his attention was drawn to Lila's skilled preparation.

Eli scribbled numbers on a piece of paper he'd pulled from his pocket. "I can make ten dollars a week next summer when I work full-time! That pays for a year's tuition at Ohio State."

"No way! What will you do?"

Mrs. Stoff looked up and smiled at Hershel. "Exactly what I'd like to know."

"I get to fix the engine blocks of Chevrolets. I used to tinker with car parts back in Vienna." Eli picked at the apple strudel cooling on the counter before he turned and walked out.

Hershel followed him. "Then when you gonna have time for the movies?"

∞∞∞

IT BECAME A SUNDAY-AFTERNOON ritual that spring. Hershel and Eli would go over to the 571 Shop, and one of their mothers would cut them each a slice of *Sachertorte*, which they'd savor with a glass of milk in the kitchen. Hershel watched Eli separate the two layers of chocolate sponge, scraping his fork over the apricot jam and eating it first. "Don't you find that too sweet?" Hershel asked him. Eli just smiled, licking his lips, gulping down half the milk. "It's no different than the glob of whipped cream you just piled on top."

From the bakery they'd head to The Main Street Theatre for the featured film. Eli used the movies to perfect his English and learn more about American customs and mannerisms. It was clear he wanted to assimilate. Hershel liked being Eli's trusted advisor.

One afternoon they saw *The Crowd Roars*. They figured they'd enjoy it because it was about boxing. Afterward, both boys agreed that Robert Taylor and Maureen O'Sullivan were good actors. They liked when the audience stood up out of their seats applauding Tommy McCoy's knockout punch to his opponent in the eighth round, having endured a merciless pounding to throw the fight when he thought it would save his girlfriend.

Hershel sensed some discomfort from Eli, who seemed lost in thought as they left the cinema. He nudged his friend with an elbow. "What'd you think?"

"That side of life—I've never seen it before." Eli scrunched his face in concentration. "What would you call it, the seedy side? Kinda caught me off guard, I guess. The gambling, the drinking. Other stuff too."

"Yeah, maybe I'm more used to it 'cause of all the movies I've seen here. A bunch of old gangster films—*Scarface*, *City Streets*. There was that one—*Angels with Dirty Faces*—that just came out with James Cagney—"

"Who's he?"

"This great tough-guy actor. Plays gangsters a lot. Has a thick New York accent. Pretty intense."

"Would I like it?"

Hershel replayed the plot in his head. "It takes place in a real bad New York neighborhood—Hell's Kitchen. It's about two friends on different paths. One becomes a priest." He paused for a few seconds, watching something inscrutable flicker across Eli's face. "It's a good story."

∞∞∞

THE NEXT WEEK THEY headed to the theater for a double feature: *Boys Town*, with Spencer Tracy and Mickey Rooney, two of Hershel's favorite actors, and *The Adventures of Tom Sawyer*. Hershel gave Eli the Mark Twain book to read in advance. "It'll help your English too," he'd told him. Afterward, Eli said he learned much more than language: here was a typical American boy during the mid-nineteenth century. The small-town setting was also an eye-opener.

The boys bounded for the front and grabbed seats in the first row. Eli opened a box of Jujubes.

Hershel leaned over and whispered, "You have a real sweet tooth!"

"My Viennese upbringing." Eli grinned as he popped the gummy candy in his mouth. Hershel held out his hand while Eli shook a few pieces free.

Throughout the theater, lighters flickered on and off like fireflies in summer fields. Then the screen lit up with *The*

Adventures of Tom Sawyer. The boys stretched their necks back, gazing at the faces of the actors, their outsized mouths talking back and forth.

Once the film was over, Eli spouted off many reactions. "I don't get why they had to change the way Injun Joe dies."

"The movies just try to make things real . . . real dramatic, you know?" Hershel had seen so many that he felt like an expert. "It's way more exciting for Tom to kick Injun Joe so he falls to his death than for Injun Joe to get lost in the cave and just die of starvation."

"I guess you're right." Eli furrowed his brows, then started mumbling. "M-i-s-s-i-s-s-i-p-p-i. Miss-is-sip-pi. I love to spell it, I love to say it, I love how the word sounds. And I loved Tom and Huck's wild ride down the river."

Hershel thought Eli's reactions were funny. It was almost like the weird things his brother, Meyer, came up with when he was little. But it was different hearing it from someone his own age. He was impressed with Eli's ability to read and speak as well as he could in a foreign language, though.

"How many years did you study English in Austria?"

"It was part of the curriculum since *Realgymnasium.* That's the school you start when you're ten, maybe eleven. I never thought it'd become my main language."

Hershel was about to compliment Eli's diction when the lights dimmed for the second feature and the opening credits started scrolling. Spencer Tracy played Father Edward Flanagan, a priest who in real life started a group home called Boys Town for underprivileged and delinquent boys in Omaha, Nebraska. Rooney played one of the boys Flanagan took in, Whitey Marsh, a tough-talking hoodlum. Hershel wondered if Eli would pick up all the slang and awaited his usual torrent of questions.

The lights hadn't even been turned up when Eli asked, "So what does *sucker* mean? Whitey's campaign slogan was 'Don't be a sucker.'"

"It's just . . . I don't know. A way people talk." Hershel got up from his seat, as did Eli, and the two walked up the aisle, squinting as the lights went on. "Someone who believes whatever they hear, that's a sucker."

"And do American people actually use *ain't*? It's not a proper word, right?"

"I wouldn't use it at Central High, if that's what you're asking." Hershel gave Eli one of his friendly punches as the two entered the lobby with the movie crowd, emptying with it onto the sidewalk and into the night.

They walked quietly, absorbed in their own thoughts. They passed a closed pharmacy and butcher shop, their eyes straying toward the hardware store, also dark inside, before they crossed Main Street. Eli finally broke the silence. "You know, I really liked *Boys Town*."

"I did too. What'd you like best?"

"The good will of the priest. That he cared about saving the lives of those boys."

"Yeah. And it's a true story. I mean, this guy really exists."

"You know, I wouldn't be in America if it wasn't for a man like that, who cared about saving people's lives. He vouched for my family and never even met us." Eli went quiet again for a minute. "I want to meet him someday. And thank him. If not for him, I'd never have met you, Hershel."

∞∞∞

By late May, Eli's mother found a Jewish landlord who would rent the Stoffs an apartment. It was a couple blocks from the Goldsteins, near their synagogue on Bryden Road. The red brick building was divided into four apartments, two upstairs and two down. The Stoffs moved into one on the bottom floor the week after Eli's Central High graduation. Like many of the houses in the neighborhood, it had a front porch that entered into the living room. Past that were two bedrooms off a short hallway, with the kitchen in the rear. Mr. and Mrs. Stoff set up a card table in the living room so the Goldsteins could come over for their weekly canasta night. The boys started using it, too, for bridge and pinochle.

One Sunday, Hershel, Eli, and Max Sherman had trouble finding a fourth for bridge and recruited ten-year-old Meyer for the dummy hand. Meyer squirmed in the chair, red-faced and clearly aggravated at being called "dummy."

"It's just a player designation. Don't take it personally, Meyer." Hershel dealt thirteen cards facedown to each player. He reminded Meyer how to count his points based on the high cards and suits, and he tried to subtly learn what cards his brother was holding in the process. Meyer's baby fat and inability to pay attention belied the fact that he was a math whiz. While everyone was still arranging their cards, Hershel announced an opening bid of "three no trump."

Eli nodded across the table to Max. "Don't be a sucker."

Hershel tried to hold in a grin, impressed that Eli correctly incorporated the slang in suggesting to Max that Hershel was bluffing.

Max bid four hearts, Hershel instructed Meyer to pass, Eli passed as did Hershel, and the bidding contract was established with Max taking the lead. The game ended with Eli and Max one hand short of their bid just as aromas from the kitchen wafted over them.

"Let's take a break and visit with your parents," Hershel suggested. In quick succession, Hershel collected and shuffled the cards, stacked them in the center of the table, pushed out his chair, and headed toward the back of the apartment. He knew his priorities.

Eli, Max, and Meyer followed close behind. They found Mr. and Mrs. Stoff deep in conversation—in German—that Eli had no qualms interrupting. "Okay for us to get a snack, Mama?"

Hershel noticed Eli's discomfort whenever his parents spoke German. Mrs. Stoff must have been aware of this because she immediately shifted to English. "Sit down, boys. I've made a fresh batch of Viennese fingers."

The elongated butter cookies were covered with chocolate at both ends. Hershel scooped up a piece, still warm to the touch and practically crumbling in his hand. He popped it in whole, groaning with pleasure as it melted in his mouth. "Mrs. Stoff, you are an artist!"

Eli rolled his eyes. "And you say I have a sweet tooth." After motioning to Meyer and Max to help themselves, he turned to his mom. "What were you and Papa saying . . . about downtown and some neighborhood?"

"Papa took the bus downtown to a hardware store last week, and he discovered a German neighborhood."

"Oh, that's German Village, Mrs. Stoff." Hershel had visited the area when he was younger with his mother as she was starting up the 571 Shop. They'd gone to several bakeries there so she could observe how they were run and what items seemed to sell best. He remembered the many German-speaking people, all of whom seemed to know one another.

"*Viele* of the *Volk*—" Bart Stoff nervously smoothed his hand over his bald head and looked toward his wife. "I know. I need to *sprechen Englisch*." He furrowed his brow and continued. "Many of the people in my work . . . at the stockroom . . . are from Germany and they live in this *Dorf*, this village."

"Your papa was telling me that a lot of German immigrants settled there in the early 1800s. They worked hard,

opened up shops, and soon a third of the population of Columbus was German. They built businesses, schools, and churches.
Obviously, these people are not Jewish."

Mrs. Stoff paused then, as if she was trying to choose her
next words carefully. "I don't want to sound like an alarmist—
these local Germans have lived here for quite a while. But there
are troubling signs in Europe that are hard for us, as Jews, to
ignore. It's why we left. And it's getting worse."

Meyer didn't seem to be listening as he placed two more
cookies onto his plate. Hershel, Eli, and Max nodded self-
consciously.

"I've been called some pretty nasty names by kids at
school," Max said, shuffling from one foot to the other.

"Yes, but we are safe here." Mrs. Stoff smiled tenderly
at Max.

"What about that ship carrying Jewish refugees that sailed
here from Hamburg last month? The U.S. refused to admit
them as citizens, and they had to go back. What will happen
to them?"

Eli's pressing questions were met with silence. Hershel
wasn't completely surprised by this impassioned side of his
friend. He'd seen it in his reaction to the work of the priest
in *Boys Town*. As their relationship deepened, Hershel had
observed a trait of Eli's that made him different—in a good
way—a quality he couldn't quite describe. Hershel tried to
understand what life had been like in Vienna, but Eli didn't
talk much about it, at least not about how he felt. And now
he realized Eli had been keeping abreast of news from Europe
far more than any of their American-born Jewish friends. Even
more than Hershel's parents. Hershel wondered if they were all
living in some bubble of willful ignorance.

∞∞

As SUMMER DREW TO a close, Hershel dreaded returning to Central High without Eli. True to his word, Eli earned his hundred dollars for a year of college tuition working that whole summer in the junkyard, still making time to play bridge and check out the latest movies.

Days before school began that September, word of a war in Europe started dominating the news and their conversations. They learned that Germany attacked Poland, the Germans portraying it as an act of self-defense after an alleged assault by Poles on a radio station in a Silesian city called Gleiwitz. In short order, England and France declared war on Germany. A cloud seemed to hover over their east-end neighborhood. As Hershel began his senior year of high school, Eli decided to delay college for a year and continue working at the junkyard. Hershel was glad Eli still lived around the corner and that the two could spend their free hours together.

By mid-month, they read that the Soviet Army had invaded Poland from the east. By the end of September, Poland fell under the control of Germany and the Soviet Union. Hershel got most of his information from Eli, who seemed to know people with connections on the east coast, where news about the war was far steadier than the dribble of articles in the Columbus papers. By November, sparse coverage was coming from the front lines, and all the newspapers began referring to the war in Europe as the "Phony War" because it seemed like nothing was happening.

Meanwhile, the Stoffs, who had been agnostic in Austria, joined the Bryden Road Temple, where all Jews from the east end belonged. There, Rabbi Zelkowitz would include bits of war news not found in the papers in his Friday-night sermons. Mrs. Stoff said she was eager to learn as much as possible about the situation in Europe, often talking to Hershel and Eli about her mother, who'd stayed behind. She translated a few of the letters she received—*Aunt Miriam's baking makes you look like Franz Sacher. . . . It's a good thing my hearing's gotten worse so I miss most of the bad news on the radio*—leaving Hershel feeling like he almost knew Eli's grandmother, a composed woman who seemed to master all the circumstances life dealt her. Given the uncertainty of the times and her own anxious worry, Mrs. Stoff voiced the importance of being engaged in the community. She decided to join the temple choir.

∞

IN EARLY DECEMBER, THE Stoffs invited the Goldsteins to join them for an early Shabbat dinner at their apartment, followed by a Chanukah service. While he didn't particularly like going to synagogue services, Hershel was happy to spend an evening with Eli and his family. After the mothers lit the *Shabbos* candles, Mrs. Stoff served Hershel's favorite food: *Wiener Schnitzel*, a freshly baked challah, and apple strudel for dessert.

The chill of winter was already in the air as they walked the three blocks to temple. Hershel was surprised to find the chapel filled to capacity—about a hundred people. After the regular service and once the choir finished "I Have a Little Dreidel" and "Oh Chanukah," Rabbi Zelkowitz wasted no time getting into the meat of his sermon: rumors he heard from several sources that the Nazis had deported Jews from Austria to Poland. Hershel looked around the chapel and saw the rabbi had the congregants' rapt attention.

"I can't be positive, of course, but that's the report I'm getting." The rabbi stroked his beard and paused. "Which begs the question. Why?"

Hershel's eyes landed on Mrs. Stoff, seated among the choir members, just as she gasped loudly enough to be heard. The rabbi went on to share a British government report about what he called concentration camps being built in Europe for Jews and anti-Nazis resisters. He also said there were accounts of Polish Jews being ordered to wear Star of David armbands. At this point, audible groans could be heard throughout the small chapel.

Hershel's head felt heavy as they left the synagogue. He broke the silence, addressing no one in particular. "Why don't we hear anything the rabbi said at school or read about it in the papers?"

"I guess no one knows for sure, Hershel." His father put his arm over Hershel's shoulder. "The rabbi did say they were rumors."

Eli kicked a stone off the sidewalk. "Or maybe if the truth gets out, our country has to do something, and it would rather sit on the sidelines."

Hershel wondered what it would take for America to get involved. All of this seemed so far away to him. So unreal. Like watching a movie and getting lost in the action, but then as the lights go up, you can walk out. Remind yourself it's only a story.

Hershel looked back at Eli and then at his father. He wasn't sure how long he could hold onto that comfort.

Part Two

ENLISTMENT

Early 1943

CASABLANCA WAS ELI'S SUGGESTION for Saturday evening. The film had captured the country's attention when it premiered last Thanksgiving, just as the Allies invaded North Africa. He'd read all about it: an American expat and former freedom fighter caught between his love for a woman and his desire to help her and her rebel Czech husband escape the Germans from the Vichy-controlled city of Casablanca; the steamy pairing of Humphrey Bogart and Ingrid Bergman. He couldn't wait to see it, and tonight it opened in theaters across the country. The Loew's Ohio added extra night showings to accommodate war-plant shift workers, making it easier for Eli and Hershel to fit the movie into their college schedules.

As he walked across the Oval to meet Hershel at the student union, Eli found himself among a gathering of people in trench coats, umbrellas in hand. The temperature hadn't dipped down to freezing even though it was the third week in January. The crowd's eyes were on a slow-moving float with the sign "Weld Your Way to Victory" stretched across the tractor bed, held up at both ends by students tottering with each small bump in the pavement. Eli asked an onlooker what was going on. "Engineer's Day Parade," the man told him. "Seemed good to focus this year's theme on the war," he shouted above the commotion.

No doubt about it: war was in the air. By the summer of 1940, Germany had conquered France, and that September the U.S. established the Selective Training and Service Act—the first peacetime draft in the country's history. All men twenty-one to forty-five had to register. But then came Pearl Harbor, and just last November, with the war at its height, the Act was amended to lower the age to eighteen. Eli, at nineteen, was now eligible. He and everyone he knew became preoccupied with the draft and everything having to do with it.

With winter-quarter midterms just a week away, the film was the perfect diversion from studying. Movies at the downtown Loew's became a weekly event for the two while Hershel finished high school and Eli worked full-time. Eli had been in no hurry to begin college at age sixteen, having tested into his senior year when he arrived in Columbus. Now, the friends rode the bus together from campus like they used to from their east-side neighborhood to Central High. Eli couldn't believe their junior year at Ohio State was halfway over already.

Hershel sat right next to Eli in the back of the crowded bus, both bundled in winter coats, their book bags on their laps. "Do you remember when we first started going to the movies?" Eli asked him, smiling as he thought back to their Sunday-afternoon ritual that first year he arrived from Vienna.

"How could I forget? And think how quickly your English improved."

"Yeah, but now my accent is barely noticeable. You agree?" Eli bumped his shoulder affectionately against Hershel's.

The bus dropped them across the street from the Loew's. Walking through the theater lobby, they passed promotions for war bonds. "What if Garrett is drafted?" Hershel was referring to Roger Garrett, who played the Robert Morton pipe organ, a famed Loew's attraction.

Eli preferred the occasional live appearances by stars like Judy Garland and Jean Harlow over the uninspiring musician. "How do you know he isn't an enlisted reserve but hasn't been called up yet? I read there aren't enough training facilities for everyone who's now eligible." He was more concerned with his own draft status than that of the organist.

Eli moved past the line of people waiting to purchase war bonds and joined the long queue for popcorn. He told Hershel to get them tickets and seats and gestured him to go on. In an afterthought, he called after him, "You want yours buttered?" Hershel's head bobbed as he kept walking.

Last fall, Eli found himself mired in ambivalence. Should he enlist or wait for the Draft Board notice? Enlistees got a say about which branch of service they wanted, and even the specialty within that chosen branch. Draftees were assigned wherever the Draft Board saw the most need—likely the Army infantry, where he wanted to be assigned anyway. To Eli, enlisting was a voluntary act that fit with his desire to give back to his new country. And yet his real aspiration was to complete his education. War unmade one's plans. War created uncertainty.

Three students he recognized from his business classes stood farther up in the popcorn line. Eli nodded to them in greeting. He couldn't help eavesdropping, their voices carrying over the lobby's general tumult. There was no mistaking their eagerness to leave college and join the war effort. He understood their fervor. Here was a chance to make a difference. For one's life to have real purpose.

"All these American boys want to fight. Good for them. Good for this country. Good for the world," his mother had told him in December as the deadline for voluntary enlistment was nearing. "But you need to finish school." She'd wrung her hands as she spoke, her voice rising in pitch. "I can't risk losing you too."

That last word—*too*—hung heavy in the air between them. Anxiety and guilt had continued to plague his mother since their escape from Vienna five years earlier. Their hope to get Gramma Jenny out evaporated after they lost touch with her a year later. Eli had heard all the rumors about the destruction of Jewish homes and businesses and the deportations of Jews. They all had. But it was easier to write it off as war hysteria. Until they couldn't. After Pearl Harbor, with national radio broadcasts reporting on the fighting three times a day, Eli watched his mother drop everything to listen. At the bakery, she and other refugee women discussed the latest reports. Any announced casualties put her into a tailspin.

"Lila, *was ist, wird sein*," Eli's father would tell her. *What will be, will be.* His father had become the less dominant parent because of his struggles acclimating to American life, nearly fifty when they arrived here. But during this tense time, Papa emerged as a calming influence. He'd always accepted his fate and moved on. When his small uniform company in Vienna was seized because of Hitler's racial policies, he found piecemeal work to get them by until their well-timed departure. His continued difficulty with English stuck him with low-level work in Columbus, yet he remained affable and steady.

"Papa's right. I may not have a choice," Eli had told his mother. To calm her fears, he shared with her what he'd gleaned from the student newspaper: that he wouldn't get drafted until February or March and likely be permitted to finish the school year. He had figured, back then, he'd have at least a six-month reprieve.

"Hey, did ya hear me?" The youngest of the OSU students had popped up beside Eli.

"Sorry. Did you ask me a question?" Eli noticed a pin on the boy's jacket lapel, a sterling silver eagle spread across the V symbol.

"Just wondering what branch you signed up for."

Eli shrugged. In dragging his feet, he felt at odds with his own conscience and with most of the country. "Haven't formally enlisted. You?"

"I asked for the Marines, but I just want in." Under his breath he added, "I'm actually only seventeen but wrote I was eighteen to register."

Eli forced a half smile before the guy turned back to his friends. After Pearl Harbor, young men lied about their age so they could get drafted. The appetite for all things war-related was insatiable. He recalled the recent ads promoting war bonds as "the best Christmas present for any American" prominently positioned down the street by Lazarus on Town and High, along with the store's promotions for its Army officer uniforms. Still, something had held Eli back. And before he could commit, voluntary enlistment closed.

So here he was, waiting to get his official draft letter. Eli paid a dime for the two bags of popcorn and hurried down the aisle just as a newsreel headline filled the screen: "Everyone Joins The U.S. War Effort." Spotting Hershel, he slid into the row, preparing to lose himself in that familiar darkness.

∞∞∞

THE FOLLOWING FRIDAY NIGHT, Eli, Hershel, Lenny Levine, Charlie Markowitz, and Kenny Shulman piled into Eli's '36 Chevy. The talk on the drive from campus was all about Ohio State football despite the fact that now, halfway into winter quarter, the season was almost a distant memory. Eli knew that football gave them an emotional outlet and that talking about it meant they didn't have to discuss their uncertain futures. They were heading to the annual youth service at Bryden Road Temple, all likely as surprised as Eli was that this year's featured speaker was Ohio State's president, Howard Bevis. Eli expected to see familiar faces in the crowd since all the Jewish youth in town and on campus were invited, including his fellow Hillel members and the Jewish fraternities and sororities. The dance that followed the lecture was clearly the biggest attraction.

Other than Eli and Hershel, Lenny was the only boy from the Columbus vicinity. Kenny was from Brooklyn, Charlie from Cleveland. They'd all met their freshman year at a Friday Firesides Hillel gathering.

"Chuck Csuri was elected Buckeye captain for the fall." Kenny was a walk-on and had attended the football banquet a few weeks earlier. "Csuri's a good guy. Great tackle."

"I think Gene Fekete drove us to victory." Charlie was the least athletic of the group but the most well-read on all sports. "And he's just a sophomore, so we'll have two more years with him at fullback."

"You think Bevis will talk about football tonight?" Lenny yawned.

"Are we keeping you up, Levine?" Kenny jabbed Lenny, and they all laughed. "How'd you get this jalopy, Stoff?"

"I worked at a junkyard. Fixed engine blocks." Eli put on his right blinker as they approached the temple. "Paid my tuition plus let me buy this cheap and rebuild it." As a commuter student, he liked the idea of having a car, especially to haul around his friends on weekend nights like this. He thought the vehicle was a beauty despite Kenny's wisecrack.

The boys took their seats in the back of the synagogue. Eli scanned the crowd of students just as Hershel elbowed him, nodding toward several girls a few rows up on the right of the aisle. He'd seen a few of them around Hillel but didn't know their names. Trying to ignore the whispers and snickers from his friends, he picked up the prayer book.

After an abbreviated religious service, Rabbi Zelkowitz introduced President Bevis. To loud applause, Bevis approached the dais, his tall frame and erect posture making him appear younger than his fifty-seven years, despite a receding hairline. Bevis was well-liked, often seen talking with students on the Oval. Eli especially admired that he'd taught both law and business administration at Harvard, and that he had served in the First World War, in Army ordnance.

As expected, the lecture began with football—accolades for last season's winning team, the exceptional student athletes, the top-notch marching band—but quickly moved to the topic on everyone's mind. Winning the war became the pressing goal of the entire campus community after the Japanese attack on Pearl Harbor, Bevis reminded the audience. "Schools take their places alongside factories and training camps as necessary agencies of preparation for battle." He acknowledged that the war was already dominating the life and priorities on campus. He announced that Ohio State was one of six schools to join the Midwest War Council, a college consortium to coordinate members' war efforts and disseminate information. He quoted FDR, who'd predicted that 1943 carried the promise of a "very substantial advance along the roads that lead to Berlin, Rome, and Tokyo" and complimented the strong offensives by Soviet armies. Bevis noted that while FDR wouldn't say where or when the next land strike in Europe would be, the president promised that the U.S., Britain, and the Soviet Union would "hit them from the air heavily and relentlessly."

As the students dispersed into the social hall, Lenny suggested they get in line for the fruit punch. Talk of the war surrounded them. Ahead someone was mentioning the ROTC training he saw that morning near University Hall. "They were using an anti-aircraft gun," the student asserted.

"I just read in *The Lantern* that the Soviets gained on all fronts and got the Nazis to retreat fifty miles," Eli announced to no one in particular. "I think the war is turning in the Allies' favor." He felt uplifted by the lecture. As though victory might be around the corner, as though this war wasn't as endless as the reports made it sound.

"Look, I think we need to finish the job, not to mention ridding the world of anti-Semitism," Kenny pronounced. As an engineering major, he would likely receive a deferment.

"You saying there's stuff going on here?" Lenny grabbed a glass mug and began filling it with punch.

"You know I'm a member of the Ohio Staters," Charlie said. "During one of our campus cleanups, we found a swastika painted on a wall outside the ZBT house."

"Don't you think that's an isolated case?" Hershel asked.

"Not sure. I just saw something in the classifieds in *The Lantern* that made me wonder. Ad sought a male student—white and gentile, it said—to do odd jobs in exchange for a room and meals." Charlie frowned. "There will always be people who are uncomfortable around those unlike them. Racism, anti-Semitism—it all stems from fear. That's what I think."

"Hey, let's mingle and leave all that for the real adults," Hershel suggested. He took his mug and walked toward a tight circle of girls from AEPhi. Eli followed him.

∞∞

ELI DIDN'T WANT TO attend the "Music in Wartime" series alone. The OSU Symphony Orchestra was scheduled to perform the second Sunday afternoon in February in the men's gymnasium. Sibelius and Schubert, two longtime favorites, got his attention. Now he had to get Hershel's.

"Rebecca might enjoy it. Ask her to come."

Hershel had met Rebecca Hoffman at the youth service reception, and he was clearly smitten. Eli reminded Hershel that Rebecca was a music major who played the cello, so he would score points for suggesting the outing. As it turned out, Rebecca asked to bring her friend, Elaine Friedman, who also loved concerts. The fact that the new series, directed by Rebecca's beloved professor, Eugene Weigel, was dedicated to the Red Cross, the War Bond Campaign, and other patriotic causes made the appeal even stronger.

After the concert, the four headed to the university bookstore in the east basement of Derby Hall. They forgot it was closed on weekends, but they passed a classroom in use this Sunday. The sign outside the door read: "Navy Recognition School." Eli had heard about the intense training program when he donated blood at the High Street Red Cross headquarters. He explained that soldiers were being taught vision and perception exercises to help identify aircraft as enemy or friendly. Elaine cast an admiring glance Eli's way. Pretending not to notice, he kept walking down the hall toward the exit door.

They strode east through campus. Crossing the Oval, Hershel asked if they wanted to get a snack at the Ohio Union Grill.

"That place is too noisy, and I can't stand the smell around the cigar counter." Rebecca scrunched up her nose for effect. "How about we get food at Hillel?"

They passed several boys wearing freshman beanie caps. Elaine said she thought they looked silly. Rebecca observed there seemed to be fewer males on campus this year. They exhaled frosted air when they spoke.

The student canteen at Hillel wasn't busy. Eli ordered four bagels with cream cheese and four hot chocolates as the others scanned the event calendar on the message board behind them. "*Sons of Liberty* is showing upstairs at seven," Rebecca announced. "Along with the usual short subjects on the war, of course."

"Why do they offer such obscure films?" Hershel asked as he took both his and Rebecca's trays and set them down in a nearby booth.

"Actually, it's a 1939 American drama about a Polish-born American businessman named Haym Salomon," Elaine explained. "He was the prime financier of the American side during the Revolutionary War against Great Britain."

When Hershel rolled his eyes, Eli felt he had to defend Elaine. "Only a history major would know these details. Hershel and I love going to movies." He took a bite of his bagel.

"And I'm taking world history this quarter." She smiled gratefully at Eli. "I also happen to like films. *Sons of Liberty* won an Academy Award for Best Short Subject."

"Academy Award aside, I'd rather not wait an hour for that. We could head to the student union to get tickets to the Military Ball. It's next Saturday night at the men's gym." This time it was Eli's turn to eyeball Hershel, who was undaunted. "Tommy Tucker and his orchestra are playing, just three bucks including tax. 'Dance Your Way to Victory' theme. Sounds like a blast."

"I think it *would* be fun." Rebecca pushed her plate away and slid her arm inside Hershel's elbow.

"So, let's go." Hershel was the first to get up, taking their trays to the counter.

They grabbed their coats and returned to the early evening's chill. "As long as we're making plans, why don't we go to the junior prom?" Eli was really asking Elaine but directed it to all of them. He was a member of Bucket and Dipper, the junior men's honorary. His high grades and service with Student War Activity Volunteers got him in. "The junior and senior proms will be held together this year. And it was moved up to early March since so many enlisted reserves will likely leave school at the end of the quarter."

"I'd love to go with you, Eli." Elaine then turned to Rebecca. "We need dresses. I hear the Union now has a campus shop on High Street with reasonable prices. Want to head there after classes tomorrow?"

∞∞∞

ELI PULLED UP THE collar of his wool overcoat as he left Haggerty Hall for the Main Library to meet Hershel between classes. It was the first of March, the final week of winter quarter with the junior-senior prom that Friday night. *Get in the moonlight mood at the final prom for the duration!* the promotions exclaimed, with moonlight, instead of war, as the theme of the dance. A welcome respite, given the quickening pace of academic life in wartime, with classrooms filled from morning to late evening so students could take a full rotation of courses in nine instead of twelve months. Draft notices were trickling out, and many of Eli's friends, except those in majors like premed or engineering or agriculture, had the jitters awaiting their orders.

Eli read that Ohio State, like many land-grant universities, signed contracts with the War Department for Army Specialized Training Programs. The university hosted several for the military. They adjusted curriculum to fit the needs created by war. Specialized topics within engineering and science courses, management war training, and language classes in Russian and Japanese appeared for the first time, as did aeronautical meteorology, military geology, and the interpretation of maps for military purposes. Soldiers also studied medicine, veterinary medicine, and dentistry. There were so many soldiers on the Ohio State campus that the Army provided a shuttle between downtown's Union Station, where the trains came in, and the stadium dormitories, where the cadets resided. As he approached University Hall, Eli stood aside when at least a hundred uniformed soldiers doing synchronized exercises marched past. The reality of the draft was always in front of him. It was just a matter of time before he and Hershel were part of it.

Entering the library, Eli stopped outside the War Information Center on the first floor. A poster showing a wounded lieutenant staggering toward his comrades caught his eye. *What are you doing for the war, brother?* the poster asked. Another placard advertised the Red Cross Carnival, to be held that evening in the men's gymnasium, the kickoff for a full campus fund drive to benefit the war effort. Admission was only fifty cents and entered the ticket holder into a drawing for two twenty-five-dollar war bonds as door prizes.

Eli's letter from the Draft Board had arrived two weeks earlier, a week after Hershel got his. When he came home that day, he found his parents tuned into a WOSU radio broadcast on the Mutual Network devoted to the works of Beethoven. The Fifth Symphony's rhythmic opening phrase—"dit-dit-dit-dah"—cheerily welcomed him along with the official notice, which began, "Greetings . . ." As his father had prepared them all, "What will be, will be." The draft order was not unexpected.

And his physical was two days from now. Climbing the library stairs, he wondered about Hershel's, which had taken place that morning. Eli avoided doctors in general, squeamish about medical exams, and he sought his friend's assurances. He found Hershel in the adjacent study space. He set his satchel of books on the table. "Hey. You done studying yet?"

"Just accounting test left to review. I'm good."

"So what happened?"

"What do you mean?"

"At your physical, nincompoop."

"Can you believe it? I got 4-F. Flat feet."

It took a few beats for Eli to grasp the significance of Hershel's words. He stood still for a moment to catch his breath, to process the news. He felt happiness for Hershel in the next instant—happy that Hershel's plans would not be disrupted by war, that Hershel's future could move forward. But then he thought about his own situation and felt suddenly empty, unmoored. He'd be going overseas; he'd lose touch with Hershel for what could be years. He'd be far from his home and family.

But he said none of this to Hershel. His default reaction was always to keep things light. "With those flat feet, I hope you'll be able to handle Rebecca Friday night on the dance floor."

∞∞

"Ooooh!" Rebecca squealed in delight as they stepped into a transformed gymnasium. Stars and half-moons, twinkly lights, and blue balloon centerpieces created a magical scene.

Elaine lifted her gown hem as she maneuvered the two steps into the ballroom, Eli offering her his arm. The soft sounds of clarinets and trumpets played the familiar tune, "Moonglow," as the two couples made their way inside, their eyes adjusting to the dimmer lighting.

The fourteen-piece orchestra began playing "Life Goes to a Party" at full volume. At its conclusion, a shrill voice over the intercom introduced the junior and senior class presidents, along with their dates, for the first dance. "Sing, Sing, Sing" quickly followed, and the surrounding crowd of watchers were encouraged to join them out on the floor. Eli winked over at Hershel.

The orchestra had a sensational style, bridging the gap between the extremes of sweet and swing—a combination of Glenn Miller and Benny Goodman. After Eli and Elaine and

Hershel and Rebecca danced through "Moonlight Serenade" and "In the Mood," they moved to the bar and dessert buffet, then found a table far enough from the dance floor where they could talk. Spring-quarter class choices briefly took over the conversation until they returned to the subject of war. Eli stayed quiet, forking a large bite of chocolate cake into his mouth. He'd passed his physical that morning and was thinking about that as Hershel broke his own news to Rebecca.

"You're not eligible? That's a relief!" There were girls on campus who wouldn't date boys who failed their physicals, but Rebecca wasn't one of them. "I heard that a solid third are rejected for physical ailments—even a hernia or being hard of hearing are classified."

Eli told them he passed and quickly added, "You're lucky Hershel didn't step on your toes on the dance floor with those flat feet of his."

"You know you're jealous, Eli," Rebecca snapped back.

"I admit, part of me wanted to be deferred. Kept thinking something could turn up in the physical and I might get a pass." Eli took a deep breath before he continued. "But a bigger part of me wants to get back there to fight the bastards who took away my country. Frankly, I find it interesting that to Americans the war only started two years ago. For me it began in '38, when my family had to escape from Vienna."

Eli looked over at Hershel, his face reddening as he realized how harsh his words sounded, sensing that Hershel was hurt. He'd never actually asked his friend how he felt about his deferment. Eli resolved to talk this through with Hershel, to apologize to him when they next were alone. For now, he took Elaine's hand and guided her to the dance floor just as the orchestra began "March Winds and April Showers."

After Eli walked Elaine back to the AEPhi House, the roar of B-17s overhead reverberated through the black night.

A shudder racked through his body. His draft letter provided his assignment: the 10th Mountain Division at Camp Hale in Colorado. But first, he'd report for basic training at the induction center in Fort Collins. He might only have two weeks left on campus.

CAMP RITCHIE

Early 1944

DESPITE THE JANUARY CHILL, Henry White and his room-mates gathered on their cabin's bare porch. The Camp Ritchie grounds—six hundred acres hidden inside the woods of west-central Maryland, ringed by the soft peaks of the Blue Ridge Mountains—felt like a resort to Henry. After all, he came from Queens.

The four—Henry, Bobby Saltman, Max Schultz, and Eli Stoff—were recent arrivals. They were about the same age—twenty, give or take. Drafted from college. But Henry was the only one born in the States. At first, all the foreign accents, especially German, made him feel peculiar, as if he'd landed in the wrong army. Yet he found it comfortable to be among several thousand servicemen. He was used to crowds.

That morning, Henry was in line to register and get his barracks assignment when he found himself standing next to three guys wearing identical fatigues, their olive duffle bags strung across their shoulders. He thought they could be brothers—each about six feet tall, solidly built, with dark hair and deep-set eyes. Eli introduced himself first, smiling with his entire face. Henry detected a German tinge in the way Eli pronounced *Coolumbus, Ohio*. Max and Bobby held out their hands in greeting—Max lived in Detroit, Bobby nearby in Washington, D.C. They had accents, too, but theirs were barely discernible. The four reached the front of the line as a unit. That's how they wound up as roommates in Cabin One.

Most everyone at Camp Ritchie possessed some knowledge of the German language and culture. Henry considered it a prerequisite of sorts—this ability to speak, or comprehend as he did, the language of the enemy. When it was discovered, recruits got routed to Camp Ritchie on secret orders. The officers at the Military Intelligence Training Center drilled the men until they emerged as interrogators of prisoners on the front line and counter-intelligence soldiers.

After dropping off their belongings at their new living quarters, the four had headed to the mess hall. Henry felt an immediate ease and familiarity with his three cabin mates. Maybe it was that they were Jewish, as he was. He learned that at dinner, along with some details about their families and earlier lives. Henry was eager to hear more of their personal stories, sensing from their initial exchange a varying degree of persecution that brought each of them to America.

That night, as he took in the quiet beauty of their sur-roundings, Henry offered a cigarette to Eli, then lit his own. He drew in the smoke, then leaned against the wood railing and looked up at a dark sky blanketed with shimmering stars, something he never saw in the city. When he lowered his eyes, he realized that Max was holding a trumpet.

"You played long?" Henry glanced at the instrument.

"Music runs in my family. My dad was first violin with the Detroit Symphony until two years ago. The orchestra's been in a muddle since their national radio broadcasts on the Ford Symphony Hour were discontinued." Max closed his lips on the mouthpiece, pulling out his tuning slide to get a pitch, then seamlessly began playing a jazz piece Henry couldn't place. He watched Max's dexterity as he fingered the valves, how the pitch went up and down when Max pushed and pulled the tuning slide. The tune was edgy and vibrant, the notes colliding in tension. Sort of how Henry had been feeling earlier.

But now, he loosened up as the sound drew him in. They all listened, their heads moving, their feet tapping with the bebop rhythm. Max lowered his trumpet to a chorus of "Bravo!"

"Dizzy Gillespie's 'A Night in Tunisia,' right?" Bobby pulled out an old harmonica from his shirt pocket. "I can improvise with you."

Eli squinted to read the engraved script on the mouth organ's silver plating. "That's an Olympia. From Germany. You get it there?"

Bobby looked surprised at the question. "Yeah. In Hamburg. My father gave it to me just before he died, when I was ten. My mother and I emigrated to the States shortly after that. In '34. How'd you know about the make?"

Eli snuffed his cigarette on the bottom of his shoe, then dropped the butt in an empty paper cup. "I lived in Vienna until I was fifteen. So music's always been in my life too. Classical, of course. But a guy I grew up with only listened to jazz. Taught me everything about it." Eli nodded toward the harmonica. "I've had a fascination with instruments, though I don't play anything."

"I don't play an instrument either, but I know talent when I hear it." Henry sensed a deepening camaraderie among the group. "Can the two of you play together?"

"How about some Duke Ellington?" Eli motioned Henry for another cigarette.

The night air warmed with the rapid pulse of the up-tempo sounds of "Cotton Tail," the mellow "Sophisticated Lady," and the easygoing "It Don't Mean a Thing." Henry looked at his new friends—Max and Bobby jamming, Eli swaying to the beat, grinning widely—and he couldn't imagine anything as wonderful as this sound and this moment.

∞∞∞

AFTER A MONTH AT Camp Ritchie, they could anticipate the bugle call of "Reveille." Every sunrise, the abrupt sound began their daily routine: they donned their basic uniforms, straightened their cabins, and headed for the mess hall. This February morning, the sky was clear, the air cold, as Henry, Bobby, Max, and Eli followed the rows of barracks and classroom buildings lining the long street, a few officers and fellow recruits up ahead. The recent snowfall still covered the road's edges. Morning sunlight spilled through the trees, casting long shadows across their path. Henry's eyes took in the scoops of snow caught in the arms of bare trees and the frozen bushes lining the approach to their main classroom. The tall rock turrets flanking its entrance were now as familiar as the camp's history.

They'd learned that it had opened less than two years earlier, not long after U.S. forces landed in North Africa and helped drive the German Army off the continent. The government decided to centralize its intelligence operations here, near Hagerstown, Maryland, where thousands whose records indicated foreign-language fluency would receive highly specialized training: courses covering close-intelligence gathering, combat instruction, map reading, identification of enemy personnel and their armored vehicles, identification of German and other foreign aircraft. These selected recruits would become conversant in French and German and proficient in sending and receiving Morse code transmissions.

Henry found the classes at Camp Ritchie far more challenging than his three years at Queens College in Flushing, even though he'd been an accelerated student, entering in '40 at the age of sixteen, just three months after the fall of France. Along with engineering, he began studying German as part of the Army Specialized Training Program in his sophomore year. Coupled with his parents' sporadic use of German at home— they'd left Berlin after World War I—Henry gained a working grasp of the language. That and his German heritage fingered him for MI training.

In this short time, Henry and his fellow classmates had mastered the German table of organization and the Order of Battle, which covered the structure of the German Army starting with the smallest unit—the squad—and moving up through the platoon and company level of battalion, regiment, division, corps, and, finally, army. For all the divisions they might encounter in Europe, they were tested on unit designations, terms and abbreviations, the arsenal of weapons, and their chain of command. Much of the information in the courses had to be memorized because the materials, even the classroom notes, couldn't be taken with them in case they were captured. Henry still couldn't keep the dozens of variations in the specialized foreign armies straight, but he was working hard at it.

Last week they'd learned how to read foreign maps, and they'd spent hours comparing those German, French, and British versions with the U.S. ones. They learned how to make a map with a pencil, a piece of string, a clipboard, and a sheet of paper. Henry wasn't sure why this exercise was even necessary. What if they didn't have string or a clipboard out in the field? After their map-reading instruction, they had a detailed demonstration of German infantry weapons. They learned how to take apart a

German machine gun and put it together again. Eli told Henry later that he found the many details about German weaponry, and the fact that German rifles were inferior to the American models, encouraging. "We have a deep understanding of our enemy," he'd said, and had nodded at Henry with a thoughtful authority. "I think our intelligence will win the war for us."

This Monday morning, instructor Walter Lang wrote "IPW-Ge" in large bold letters on the chalkboard, short for the name of their course for the week, Interrogation of Prisoners of War—German. "How we handle prisoners of war is paramount. We're going to focus today on getting crucial information from POWs." Lang stood by the window, glancing outside. From where Henry sat, he viewed the man's profile: thick brows perpetually furrowed in lingering contemplation or inquiry, a schnoz unflattering if on a woman but considered strong or sharp on a man of his build and stature. He'd heard Lang was a career Army man. That it was his tribe and he'd joined the military right out of high school.

"There are techniques you must use to sniff out the German imposters." Lang now squarely faced the thirty trainees in the classroom. "You might find Germans who speak English so well, with no accent, that you need to trip them up. They might have forged papers and know the day's passwords. Or you might come across someone like many of you—an American who came from Germany and speaks English with a German accent, easy to mistake as an infiltrator." At that, Lang walked up the center aisle of desks and paused in front of Henry. "Ask them to recite the latest Frank Sinatra hit. Or name the team that won the World Series. Anything to finger an imposter so you don't put your life and that of your comrades in danger." He eyed the silent room of recruits. "*Verstehe?*"

After acknowledging the nodding heads, Lang added, "The detailed information you have can be used to impress prisoners. To unnerve them. Casually dropping the name of someone's commanding officer could have a profound psychological effect on a prisoner under interrogation."

He told the trainees to pair up, to reposition their desks so they faced a partner. "During this entire week, we're going to role-play to hone your skills as interrogators. One of you will be a German, the other an MI officer. I will pose scenarios, and you will act these out as if in the field. Questions before we begin?"

Max raised his hand.

"Yes, Schultz."

Max stood and saluted. "Captain Lang, I'm wondering if there's a general formula of how to begin the interrogation. So to keep the POW more willing to give us information, sir. And whether we would have weapons with us for these kinds of investigations." He sat down.

"Good questions, Schultz." Lang began to pace the room's perimeter, the sound of his clipped steps as even as a metronome. "You do not bring *any* weapons to an interrogation. That will shut down the informant before you begin." Lang looked up and made eye contact with several recruits before he continued. "Generally, you want to keep your comments circumscribed. Avoid leading questions. Most importantly, do not come off as threatening or you'll close them down.

"Of course, before a word is spoken, you should do a quick visual assessment." Lang retraced his steps, finally stopping next to the desks of Bobby and Max. "Take a prisoner's branch and rank. You can figure this out from surveying his uniform. The many insignia—the medals, ribbons, patches. Look at their boots, the piping on a cap. The uniform style. And, notably, those in the SS have the SS tattoo under their arms." The German Army Organization course taught them all of this.

Henry glanced across the desk at Eli, his sparring partner for the day. "I won't have a problem playing the evil Nazi,"

Eli whispered. "I'm sure my old schoolmates have joined the Third Reich by now."

Henry had been shocked when he first heard Eli's stories from his Vienna days. How he was ridiculed by the time he was twelve; how his father lost his small uniform store in '37 because he was Jewish. Henry realized Eli and others who grew up in Germany or Austria knew the culture and psyche of Germans better than anyone else. This innate understanding of the enemy was something less ingrained in Henry, who'd only observed the habits of his German-born parents.

As Henry began his interrogation, Eli was standing. "Grab a chair," he said. "Do you want water, or a cigarette?" He knew some instructors sought more aggressive approaches from recruits during their interrogations, but Captain Lang was not one of them. Henry felt empathy and patience was the way to face his pretend enemy.

Eli shook his head as he slid into the wooden chair, appearing a bit self-conscious in his Nazi prisoner role despite his initial bravado.

After a series of harmless questions—name, rank, serial number—Henry worked to keep his tone steady as he steered toward more sensitive tactical information. "What military unit do you belong to? Where is it located?"

Eli mumbled some kind of made-up name and setting, already acting tired of the charade.

"If you can tell me where we can find American prisoners or your bunker locations, you can be assured of our continued considerate treatment."

"I know nothing about where American POWs are held, but I can lead you to several bunkers." Then Eli began fabricating some story about a key map and his unit's next planned attack.

Before Henry could provoke Eli by suggesting his account was a lie, Lang's resounding voice announced it was time to switch places. Eli moved to the other side of the desk and Henry assumed the part of the prisoner, standing solemnly to the side. Henry watched Eli's face transform from vulnerable POW to commanding interrogator, although Eli's style was never intimidating. Henry found this exercise psychologically exhausting and energizing at the same time. Being at Camp Ritchie changed everything for him, and he knew it was the same for the others. Sure, they were far from the reaches of their parents and the scrutiny of their college friends. But here they could practice being someone else, until they *became* someone else.

As their lunch break neared, Officer Lang's booming voice again cut through the cacophony of low-pitched repartees and wrangles, and Henry's growling stomach. "When you graduate from Camp Ritchie, you will be assigned to intelligence and interrogation units attached to different outfits all over Europe. And while your value is in translation and ad hoc frontline interrogation, when needed you will fight just like any other soldier in this war." He strutted to the front of the room and turned to face them.

Henry felt the kind of drop in his gut that a sharp dip of a roller coaster used to produce. They'd be on the front lines. They'd be like any other soldier. He glanced over at Eli, trying to gauge if he caught the magnitude of this pronouncement.

∞∞

By late April, recruits in Henry's class had completed their three months of classroom instruction and began special-intelligence field activities. The combat exercises and field maneuvers created quite a stir for the farmers of west-central Maryland as, it seemed to them, German military spilled out of the woods. Henry heard the stories about complaints—the sightings of "Nazis and Japanese" and their fake Panzers "parading down" winding back roads. U.S. Army vehicles were outfitted as decoys in a reconstructed European village. If the farmers were close enough, they would have seen that the uniforms didn't fit quite right. And that the enemy soldiers in their steel helmets spoke perfect American English. Or that their dummy tanks were made of cardboard. At first, locals had no idea that their remote Maryland woodlands provided the most suitable site for top secret training. Once they learned these odd activities weren't real, Henry heard they'd tell one another, "Oh, it's just the Ritchie boys."

After sunset on a moonless night in early May, Henry and two dozen trainees were shuttled into the woods in GI trucks, a canvas cover dropped over the flatbed so they couldn't see where the drivers were taking them. The trucks left them at the edge of the forest with just a foreign map and a compass. The men's assignment was to find the trucks before daybreak. Before Henry could open his mouth to ask a question, the trucks drove off to another obscure location.

"Get a load of this map they left us." Eli kneeled on the ground and unfolded the doctored document but covered himself with a cloth so he could turn on his flashlight without it being spotted by support troops who would "shoot" him in an exercise meant to mimic actual field combat. The blanks were as loud as live ammunition. The map was always missing important details, or words—a tactic that instructors employed to make their field task more difficult. Eli strained to make out the map's distinctive markers as points of reference. He sighed. "At least it's in German."

Henry recalled last week's map written in Russian, how they couldn't hit all their checkpoints to get their envelope with tasks to complete and didn't get back to camp in the allotted time. It was the very reason they had to repeat the exercise tonight. "It's hard enough to get oriented using only a map and a compass out here. But then we can't even translate it." He stifled a yawn. "They're being easy on us tonight."

"I'm good at *speaking* German and can help with any structural document, but I can't do much with this." Max had quickly forgotten how to read German after immigrating from Frankfurt at thirteen. Army instructors were easy on him because of his understanding of architecture, his major at Wayne University. They gave him plenty of fake foreign documents of buildings and bunkers to decipher and emphasized that reading the German words wasn't crucial.

"Eli's our best bet to find our way out of here so we can *maybe* get some sleep tonight," Bobby said as he tugged at his ill-fitting Army pants. "He can read German better than the rest of us put together." Left unsaid was that Eli came to Camp Ritchie after serving a year in the Mountain Division in Colorado. They knew that of all of them, Eli Stoff was the most capable.

As Henry suspected, the evening's mission proved fairly easy. Nothing like the time a recruit on one of their field missions broke down after four hours of trekking in circles. Their MI training took its physical and emotional toll, with sleep being the antidote they desperately needed. Thanks to Eli, they got it that night at least.

∞∞

IT TOOK THEM NEARLY an hour by rail to get to Hagerstown from Camp Ritchie even though it was only eighteen miles away. They waited in the lobby of city hall for their names to be called so they could be sworn in as naturalized U.S. citizens, all but Henry, who already was a citizen. When it was Eli's turn, Henry went in with him. Eli faced an Army clerk with a stack of documents who verified his identity and said his papers were in order. The clerk handed Eli a card that he read aloud, declaring under oath that he would support and defend the Constitution and laws of the United States against all enemies, foreign and domestic, and take up arms when the nation required it. When he finished reading, the clerk stamped an official paper and handed it to Eli. "Now I'm protected if I ever become a POW," he whispered to Henry.

It was nearly seventy miles from Hagerstown to D.C., where Bobby had lived for the past ten years with his mother, Lena, and where the Cabin One crew decided to go for their three-day furlough. During the trip, Henry learned that after Bobby's father died, his mother was able to arrange exit visas because she was an American citizen by birth. Bobby had come from a prominent German family, his father a sought-after surgeon whose practice focused on facial restoration. The Salt-man home had servants. At six, Bobby attended a boarding school outside Hamburg. He told them his family was secular, although his paternal grandparents, who originally came from Romania, were observant.

"After Hitler became German chancellor, even we felt hostility." Bobby's slick black hair and dark, mysterious eyes gave him a Mediterranean look. He could have easily passed for Italian. "We had neighbors who were German diplomats. Their daughter was in school with me, and one day they invited me over. It was then I noticed a poster on their wall. 'Down with the Jewish press,' it said, and there was a swastika at the bottom. I was barely ten, but I understood what was happening."

"I guess we all had those eye-openers. Mine was six years ago." Eli gazed out the window as he continued. "It was on a train like this. I was the only Jew on a school skiing trip. My classmates were anti-Semitic, some more obvious than others. Only one boy—he was my best friend—stuck by my side. Anyway, on the ride back, Nazi soldiers appeared on station platforms at our stops in Linz and Salzburg. Turned out to be the day of the *Anschluss*. By the time I got home, my mother was desperately hunting for people to help us get out of there."

"My parents changed our name from Weiss to White when they came over from Berlin after the Great War," Henry admitted. He always felt self-conscious about admitting this fact. "I was harassed in my Queens neighborhood, so stuff wasn't always easy here either. I was a pretty scrawny kid, so when I was twelve my dad found a man who'd been a professional boxer to teach me how to defend myself. I learned boxing, wrestling, and judo—stuff in the book and not in the book. I trained three afternoons a week after school for most of that year. Alternated my bar mitzvah lessons with boxing."

He saw that the others were intently listening, so he decided to tell them about the fight. "We lived in a mixed neighborhood. Some rough older kids were always after me. One day I decided I was ready to take them on. I told the largest kid to fight me one-on-one. As he moved forward, I kicked him as hard as I could in the groin, grabbed him by the hair, and punched him hard in the stomach. He landed on his back. The others fled fast. I learned then that if you have the right tools, you can get back at the enemy. Right, fellas?"

"We all were persecuted in one way or another," Max said. "Now it's time to get even with Hitler."

They arrived in Washington in time for dinner. Bobby hadn't bothered to tell them his mother was a well-known radio host on WWDC—all the more impressive for her as a rare female in broadcasting—or that his father had socked away a bunch of money and they lived much as they had in Hamburg. And that she was a great cook.

Between bites of chicken française and rice pilaf, Lena asked what each boy had studied before getting drafted. Henry realized he'd only known about Max's expertise in architecture because it came up during document analysis class, as did his aptitude in structural engineering. Eli shared that he was a business major at Ohio State and hoped someday to attend law school.

"Mom just wants to rub in that she'd wanted me to follow my dad's footsteps into medicine. I majored in theater at George Washington—it's in Foggy Bottom. I'll take you through there tomorrow." Bobby passed the basket of rolls to Henry. "Being pre-med would have deferred me from the draft. A sore point with Mom."

"Well, then you wouldn't have met these lovely young men, Bobby. Nor would I." Lena's smile made her entire face light up.

The idea that Bobby had wanted to be an actor both surprised and made perfect sense to Henry. It explained why Bobby was exceptional during the role-playing sessions in their interrogation classes, and that he was the most sensitive of the group, prone to playing his harmonica quietly on the cabin porch. And why he seemed to dislike the intelligence field activities.

"When all this is over, I want to move to New York and perform on Broadway," Bobby confessed.

"Hey, maybe we could be roommates again." As a kid, Henry had always dreamed of building skyscrapers. That was behind his decision to major in engineering. And now he could picture it: finally getting out of Queens to live in Manhattan, working his way up at a major real estate company.

It was the first glimpse into his future that he'd let himself imagine since they met at Camp Ritchie.

∞∞∞

THE NEXT DAY, AFTER Bobby showed them around his hometown, they stopped at Lena's radio station on Connecticut Avenue. WWDC broadcast almost around the clock, beginning at eight in the morning, with newscasts five minutes before every hour. Lena hosted a daily talk show that ended at noon. She had just gotten off the air when they made their appearance.

"Well, I'm impressed. You look quite official in your Army attire." Lena led them down the station's narrow hallway, intent on giving them a tour.

Henry peeked into the first open door. "Wow! Look at all that equipment!"

A man who seemed to be in his thirties looked up at Henry, laying aside his stack of papers. A microphone speaker hung above his desk in front of a metal console filled with knobs and keys. Black padded earphones casually wrapped around his neck and rested against his crisp white collar. "Who do we have here? Well, hello, Lena."

"Wes, let me introduce you to these Army intelligence trainees—Henry White, Eli Stoff, Max Schultz. And my son, Bobby. Boys, this is Weston Karr, WWDC's top news announcer."

"Nice to meet you all." Karr pushed himself away from his desk and motioned the group to come inside his boxy studio. "I have some time before my next broadcast. Happy to answer any of your questions. But only if you share some of your military secrets with me." He flashed them his winsome smile.

Henry was most interested in the design and use of the broadcast panel. Max wondered if WWDC broadcast music as well. He shared his father's prominent role with the Detroit Symphony and that the orchestra's national radio broadcasts used to be heard on the Ford Symphony Hour. Eli and Bobby remained uncharacteristically quiet until Karr asked them questions about their Camp Ritchie training. While they avoided specifics, each spoke of the general training that would allow them to bring useful enemy information back to the Army.

A red light illuminated the glass "On Air" marquee above the door, signaling the upcoming broadcast. The trainees quickly thanked Weston for his time and filed back into the hallway. Lena corralled them into the next studio, almost identical in size and filled with similar equipment but unmanned.

"Let's listen to Weston's broadcast in here." Lena's words were cut off by her colleague's voice crackling into the studio over the intercom.

Allies land in France and wipe out big air bases! Stay tuned for more news after these words from our sponsors.

Patriotic messages filled a full minute of airtime. Advertisements for Marlboro, Nestlé, and Coca-Cola dragged on, intensifying the charged anticipation in the cramped room. Henry remained standing as he held his breath and looked at his friends, their expressions taut. This was real time. Real news. And it was coming from the studio right next to them.

After a promotion for GM's Oldsmobile division that declared "Fire power is our business," Max groused, "Geez," under his breath. Finally, Weston's voice burst back over the airwaves.

This report just in, folks. Under the command of General Eisenhower, Allied naval troops supported by strong air forces began landing Allied armies this morning on the northern coast of France. An Associated Press correspondent flying over the French coast in a B-26 Marauder reported seeing the fields inland strewn with hundreds of parachutes and dotted with gliders, while great naval forces fired into the coast fortifications. The landing fleet included several battleships, which the Germans said set the whole Seine Bay area ablaze with their fire.

No one spoke at first. But one thing was instantly, indisputably clear: their intense practice these months at Camp Ritchie was over. Henry saw resignation and acceptance as the four friends locked eyes with one another. They were ready to become intelligence experts and interrogators in a real war. To carry out their orders. But there would be the noble cause of their work and the brutal reality of that work. Didn't their instructors tell them that, in the end, war is about rage and cruelty and killing and death?

As soldiers they were about to face something immense, something they couldn't possibly grasp. It occurred to Henry how temporary their experience at Camp Ritchie had been, how fragile and fleeting their sense of belonging. He thought back to the evening on their cabin porch not six months earlier: the quiet beauty of the night and the pulsating rhythm of music that morphed into a moment of camaraderie and connection.

Who knew what uncertain fates lay ahead of them?

THE INTERROGATION

January 1945

===

BEYOND THE PRISONER FACING him, Eli Stoff saw daylight dimming through the room's single window. Across the table, the young soldier remained silent, staring at his hands, which he clasped tightly on the cold aluminum. A lighter, a broken cigarette, and a black-and-red enameled Deutsche Jungvolk membership badge lay to the side. Eli had had the boy empty his pockets before he began his interrogation. Now, several hours in, the January chill seeped through the plaster walls. It was time to get inside Malcolm Schlick's head.

Eli lowered his voice and leaned forward. "So, you had no choice but to sign on with Hitler's army. You did what you were told. I understand."

Eli was trained to "understand." He'd arrived in Paris in late December, part of a six-man military intelligence team. His orders were simple: arrest all Nazis impersonating Allied officers, put them through rudimentary questioning, write up a report. But something about Malcolm Schlick made this case more complex. Eli couldn't put his finger on it.

Schlick still wore the olive-drab uniform he'd used to blend into the Paris streets, like so many of the beaten-down Germans trying to evade capture. Last night, Eli had overheard traces of German in Schlick's otherwise fluid French as he bought a paper at the local newsstand. He noticed Schlick's uniform was scruffy, patched with dried mud—probably taken from a dead soldier. Curfew approached, so Eli had quickly motioned his MI partner, Henry White, to act as backup before he approached the likely imposter.

Now the boy—because he *was* just a boy at seventeen— sat in a sterile room in an abandoned villa in Le Vésinet, red blotches flaring up on his neck. Eli couldn't help feeling sorry for Schlick, who he now knew hailed from a village near Salzburg, plucked from his family at fifteen to face front-line combat. Whether he joined the German troops of his own volition or under duress was yet to be determined.

Eli felt a slight tapping of the boy's foot against the wood floor. "Can I get you a cup of tea or coffee?" he asked him.

Malcolm looked up, a sudden shiver twitching through his upper body. "*Ja, Kaffee. Bitte.*"

That familiar Austrian-accented German. It matched up with Schlick's Salzburg narrative.

Eli regarded the boy more closely. Malcolm was unskilled in mastering his facial expressions, lacking that mask donned by the men Eli had faced over the past weeks—a mask he would get them, eventually, to drop. Malcolm seemed unpracticed, too, in arranging his body to hide distress. Fear, not anger, shone through the young Austrian's eyes, pressing on his brows, circling his mouth. Vulnerability spoke in the slack of his shoulders.

Eli had been trained to notice these signs as he interrogated suspects and prisoners. He worked to make them feel safe so he could learn more about Nazi plans or troop movements—anything to better inform Allied forces as they edged toward victory in an insufferable war. That's how he found himself stationed in a town west of Paris, face-to-face with a member of the Hitler-Jugend just four years his junior.

Eli set down the container of coffee, its steam rising like a genie from an oil lamp. He paused while Malcolm drew the cup to his lips, then pressed on. "When did you learn French?"

"My parents sent me to private school. South of Salzburg, in Anif." Malcolm kept his head down, his sandy-colored waves falling into his face. "I learned French and English. And we had relatives in France. Visited them during summers when I was growing up."

Eli's memory of Salzburg was when he'd gone skiing in Tyrol on a class trip with his best friend, Toby Wermer, in March of '38. When he saw soldiers with Nazi banners and swastikas at the Salzburg stop on the way back to Vienna, he'd grasped his uncertain future.

"Did you ski in the winters?"

"I did. With my father. He started me when I was three." Malcolm's mouth relaxed for a moment. "But things changed . . . while I was still a young boy."

"Tell me more about how you became a soldier."

Eli went along with the boy's story that he hadn't joined the German Army of his own free will, and he purposefully didn't label Malcolm a Nazi. He knew to avoid words that might trigger the young soldier to shut down. It was part of a general avoidance of confrontation he'd learned long before his interrogation training—from all the times he'd been spat at, insulted, and bullied in his own neighborhood.

"They came to my school in '39. I was twelve. After the *Anschluss*, Hitler-Jugend membership became compulsory for us. Nazi Party reps were always coming to speak." Malcolm's eyes seemed unfocused and distant as he continued. "They talked about how Hitler's youth organization developed future officers. Made it seem an honor, a stepping-stone. There were gatherings, events. Special uniforms. Boys as young as ten were recruited. Many of my friends were excited to join."

"You weren't?" Eli remembered the pressures in Austria bubbling up and penetrating the broad consciousness of his non-Jewish neighbors, the friends of his family or the workers at his father's factory. Propaganda about the superiority of the Aryan race and against the Jews was ubiquitous. He could still see his classmates' eyes widen, taking in those uniforms in the train station on the way back from Tyrol. He understood the pull on an impressionable boy wanting to belong to something. Did Malcolm feel he had no choice? Or did he find the Nazis' message appealing?

"Let's say I had little interest in the military. I like music. I read a lot."

Of course the boy would be partial to music; after all, Salzburg was Mozart's birthplace. Music was native to Austria's air. But Malcolm's affect—the direct way he answered Eli's questions—reminded Eli of Toby. Not in appearance—Malcolm was as tall as Eli and had a sturdy build, whereas Toby was short and thin, with dark hair he wore long and unkempt. But Toby was a voracious reader of novels and any periodical he could get his hands on, and a lover of all kinds of music. He was always asking questions no one would think to articulate or making observations that would get to some truth.

"How did that go over with your friends, your teachers?"

Malcolm glanced curiously at Eli. "Not all Austrians and Germans were Nazis, you know." His eyes glared at nothing in particular. "But they made it quite clear what was the acceptable behavior and point of view. Unfortunately, most of my peers became indoctrinated. Lost their ability to see the world differently." He swallowed hard. "Boys like me knew to keep quiet or bad things would happen."

Eli remembered how Toby learned to moderate his opinions over time. Like during the Olympics in '36. Toby hated that Hitler had muddied the games, as he'd put it, with his views of Aryan supremacy. Toby voiced his thoughts within earshot of several teachers at their school. After the unannounced search of his home by local authorities that evening, Toby could only silently cheer the four gold medals won by the Negro Jesse Owens.

Toby and Eli met when they were six and became inseparable. The difference in their religious backgrounds never came up until Toby had to defend Eli.

While Eli knew there were non-Jewish Austrians like Toby who disagreed with Hitler's ideology—some who refused to join the Party—he nonetheless identified every soldier in the German Army as a Nazi. All his Army buddies did. In fact, Eli lumped all German soldiers together as the same anti-Semites who had persecuted him and his family. But Toby didn't fit this mold. And now, Malcolm Schlick didn't either. Still, Eli held onto his doubts.

"So, when Austria came under the German Reich, you joined Hitler-Jugend."

"I told you, I had to join. After '38, Austrians fell under the same Nazi laws." Malcolm pushed away from the table, the chair legs scraping the floor. "My parents signed me up the next year—they had no choice. From then on, most of Germany's and Austria's teenagers belonged to the HJ."

Eli had escaped Vienna just after the *Anschluss*, when anti-Jewish discrimination was officially sanctioned. Everything happened so fast. The affidavits came through, and his mother set straight to packing. He wrote Toby when he arrived in New York. Toby's letter back was cryptic: rapid changes in

Vienna, the omnipresence of Nazi soldiers, pressure on his parents to join the party. Then he reverted to lighthearted Toby talk—books he was reading, new jazz he'd discovered. Toby no sooner fit into the Hitler Youth movement than Eli. But that was the last time Eli had heard from him.

Eli was well aware of Nazi indoctrination but hadn't appreciated until now how systemic, pervasive, and resolute its recruitment, and how very young its members. It was something he'd emphasize in his report. But he began thinking again about Toby, just fifteen when Eli left Austria. What if he were forced, like Malcolm, to join?

"Why would you keep your membership badge, if you were coerced as you say? Pocketed as if it were a memento." The black-and-red object sat between them. Eli picked it up and turned it over, its smooth enamel surface as cold as the dank interrogation room.

"The Germans in disguise in Paris had only one enemy. I had two—the Nazis I wished to escape and the Americans who, like you, see me as a spy." Malcolm grimaced as he eyed Eli. "I needed some proof of membership if I encountered my German comrades."

Eli silently smiled at the boy's agile response and decided to veer in a new direction, beyond his standard script. "What do you remember about the *Anschluss*?"

"Germans marching into the city. Arrests. My parents said opponents of the regime and minorities were targeted—their way of urging me to keep my views to myself. A synagogue near my father's office was destroyed." Malcolm's square jaw gave him an appearance of someone older just then. He fixed his gaze on Eli. "Your German is perfect. Perfect Austrian German. When did you leave . . . and why?"

Eli should have expected this question, since nothing about this encounter followed procedure. He'd kept digging for more from Malcolm, despite the fact that he already had what he needed. He knew Schlick was a deserter from the Ardennes Counteroffensive. He had a deeper understanding of the Hitler Youth movement and new insight about the current composition of the German Army.

But it wasn't that simple now. Malcolm's enlistment had been a suffocating sentence. It was the law that he and his parents had no choice but to obey. Malcolm could have been Toby. And, if Eli hadn't been Jewish, he could have been Malcolm. A jumble of feelings roiled inside Eli. His past and present blurred in his mind, and, for a moment, he felt slightly dislocated.

Eli needed time to think. It was already late, so he chose to avoid Malcolm's question by offering to get them some food. Frosty air from the central courtyard of the villa rushed into the six-by-six space when he opened the interrogation room door. As he stepped outside, he didn't worry about Schlick escaping. The arrest seemed liberating to the boy. Like most prisoners from Germany and Austria, Schlick had to be relieved to be apprehended by the U.S. instead of the Soviets. And American treatment would easily be an improvement over the life he was trying to escape as a soldier on the front lines of a depleted army.

It felt good to be in open space, breathing in the crisp air. Eli stretched his head to one side, almost touching his shoulder, then to the other. The fading light of dusk had a calming effect on him. The villa was a safe haven, far from the battlefield and the fear they all harbored in wartime. He felt the ground, hard beneath his feet, the earth frozen solid by the frigid temperatures. Snapping sounds startled him for a moment—gunshots?—but they morphed into the crunching of footsteps just as Henry White appeared around the corner.

"How's it goin' in there?" Officially a technical specialist, White was Eli's MI partner when the two picked up Malcolm on the Paris streets.

"It . . . it's interesting." Eli stopped himself from saying more. "Can you bring us two plates from the mess hall?" Eli patted his comrade's shoulder in thanks, like a father to his son, even though Henry was less than two years younger.

He watched White's silhouette disappear into the main house, a sprawling structure shaped like a wide V. The central foyer fed into a large dining area on one side and what had become the combat regiment's main office on the other. Much of the villa's furniture had been removed and the place repurposed when Eli's MI team arrived, including the separate brick building that may have served as storage and servant quarters but was now a series of interrogation suites.

He pulled a cigarette from his pocket and lit it. As he drew the tobacco into his lungs, he thought back to when he first arrived in France. His MI team bonded well despite the clear hierarchy. Now a staff sergeant, Eli ranked below First Lieutenant Greene, Master Sergeant Landenberger, and Captain Higgins but above Henry, a T/4, and above Max Schultz, a corporal—Henry and Max were already Eli's friends from their months of training at Camp Ritchie alongside thousands of GIs, many whose native tongues were also not English. Men being groomed into interrogators of prisoners of war. It was then that Eli began to realize his knowledge of German language and culture, so long a liability, was suddenly viewed by the U.S. Army as a valuable asset. And this isolated villa became a welcome respite from the military camp in Manchester, an old, grimy textile mill town full of ancient brick factory buildings, where his unit was deployed last June. The pressure then was much higher for all of them in intelligence to help turn the tide of the war. Eli played his part; his interrogations and analysis of aerial photographs led to the identification of fortifications along the Siegfried Line and allowed U.S. troops to breech those bunkers and advance from France to Germany.

Eli exhaled smoke into the winter air. He hadn't had the luxury of private reflection, but tonight he found himself dwelling on his role as both an Austrian Jew and an Allied officer. It was easier to work steadily within the parameters of his MI training—the physical, the technical, the linguistic: interpretation of aerial codes, weeding out liars and killers, finding the enemy's secrets of war—rather than exploring his own emotions or reconciling his feelings about returning to the European fray just six years after escaping it. How he and his parents just picked up and left, how they had to abandon his grandmother in the midst of the crisis. The tears. The promises to find a way to get her later. The sadness he'd seen in his mother's eyes ever since.

Back then, Eli didn't register the finality of the family's predicament. He didn't consider that he'd never see Gramma Jenny again. Now, Malcolm Schlick was pulling him backward, to all the bullying and insults and fear of that time—but also to the lovely parts of his childhood and his special friendship with Toby. Eli had been Toby's protector, and then in that final year Toby became Eli's. Once Eli moved to the Midwest and began a new life where he was safe, he somehow let that part of his life fade away like an old photograph.

Eli had a sudden impulse and pulled out his wallet, quickly rifling through identification cards, a few American dollars, a cropped family portrait. And there it was—the discolored photo of him and Toby in Tyrol. It was so sunny that Eli had to squint to avoid the glare off the snow. Toby was in the middle of a laugh, his head tilted up toward Eli. It hit Eli then: he escaped, and Toby was left to fight as a German.

∞∞∞

"I'M A JEW," ELI said evenly.

Malcolm chewed a piece of beef, his head lowered over his plate. He took another bite before responding. "You were lucky. How'd you get out?"

"A childhood friend of my mother's lived in New York with her husband. They were poor. Didn't know the kind of people who could vouch for us." Eli hesitated, random thoughts coursing through his mind. *Also an Austrian. Also a non-Jew.* "She found a generous Jewish businessman and convinced him to take a chance on us. My parents and I got out in the nick of time. What about your family?"

Malcolm's deep-set eyes darkened. "I haven't seen them in over a year."

"Have you been in touch at all?"

"No. I was deployed as part of the Twelfth SS Panzer Division."

Eli took a deep breath as Malcolm's words sunk in. Hitler-Jugend had become Germany's military reserve. At sixteen, Malcolm was at the front line fighting a grueling war counter to his beliefs and against his will. When Eli was that age, he was completing his final year at a public high school in Columbus, Ohio.

"You said you joined the movement when you were twelve. Were there tests you had to pass? Training to become a member?"

"We had to recite all the verses of the Horst Wessel song." Malcolm began to sing, mockingly: *Die Fahne hoch! Die Reihen fest geschlossen! SA marschiert mit ruhig festem Schritt.* (The flag on high! The ranks tightly closed! The SA marches with quiet, steady step.) His voice was low-pitched, guttural.

"And . . . ?"

"We had to answer a bunch of questions about Hitler's life and about Nazi ideology and history. We ran sprints to show we were physically fit. They made us take courage tests."

"Like what?"

"I had to jump from a second-story ledge."

Eli clenched his jaw, holding back his outrage at the harsh tactics Nazis employed with mere children. He tried shutting off his anger, thinking about something else. The Camp Ritchie classroom instruction. The times they role-played to hone their skills as interrogators. Each had taken turns acting the part of a German, provoking one another with coarse words or flagrant taunts, or compelling anguish that could compromise their objectivity as they extracted information from the man facing them across the table.

"And if you refused?"

"I told you—refusal was not a choice. Failure wasn't an option." Malcolm pushed away his plate, half-eaten, placed both his hands on the table, and leaned toward Eli. "My father was severely beaten, his print shop ransacked. Just because he refused to become a member of the Nazi Party." At that, Malcolm let out a contemptuous laugh that sent a shiver down Eli's spine. "At least it kept him from being drafted. The thugs broke his leg, and it never healed properly. He was lame . . . and ineligible."

An Austrian worker persecuted in the preamble to this war. His son forced to fight against his will. Eli tried to be skeptical about what Malcolm had told him, but he kept asking himself, *How can he make up this kind of detail?* He committed to memory all the facts to include in the report. Even though the write-ups were typically brief and perfunctory, he suspected his peers shared his own ignorance.

"Tell me more about your *HJ* activities."

"By 1940 it became an auxiliary force that performed war duties. For a while I was active in fire brigades, assisted with recovery efforts. Around the Salzburg train station, mostly. Plenty of devastation resulted from Allied bombings. It kept me busy."

"So where were you deployed once you became part of the Nazi fighting forces?"

"The first major action we saw was last June during the Normandy campaign. We started with more than twenty thousand. Left with less than fourteen. As casualties mounted, members of Hitler-Jugend were recruited at younger and younger ages. Some twelve-year-olds were among the Germans' fiercest fighters."

Eli was incredulous—all his comrades would be. The Allies were fighting an army filled with virtually every teenage male in the German Reich, and some even younger. He asked himself why he trusted Malcolm. Because he was a fellow Austrian? Because he reminded Eli of Toby?

He jotted down key words in his notepad. "What happened after Normandy?"

"We were sent back to Germany, refitted; then back for the Ardennes Counteroffensive. It was brutal. Last week, after I barely dodged a bullet, I broke down. My superior officer found me huddled inside a bunker, shaking and crying. I'd wet my pants. He screamed in my ear, said to toughen up." Schlick's face was expressionless at first. Then his eyes misted over. "I was ready to die. Escape was my only hope."

Through the small window, Eli watched the evening sun sink into the horizon, a hollowness filling him. There were no rules of engagement in war. Just human beings killing one another, shooting into the darkness, and, perhaps, hitting not a man but a boy. He was glad that Malcolm had fled and their paths had crossed. His detailed report would differentiate the young Austrian from the true infiltrators and spies swarming around Paris but would likely have no consequences. Regardless, the boy would be treated well as a POW because that was the American way. Malcolm would have a future when all this was over; that knowledge gave Eli a sense of peace.

When Eli spoke again, his voice was gentle. "What do you see yourself doing? That is, if there wasn't a war."

"You know, for those of us living under Hitler, duty to the Fuhrer, the Fatherland—that was all that mattered. One's life was nothing. It's almost hard to imagine myself as separate, apart from that." Malcolm had a dreamy look in his eyes as he leaned back in his chair, his body looser, his face no longer prematurely lined. "I might be a writer. Or a musician. I guess I never had a chance to consider this. What about you?"

"When I got to America, a future opened up for me. There were many possibilities even though we were poor. Before I joined the Army, I attended a university. Studied the American system of law and the country's history."

"Will you continue your education after the war?"

Eli's life in Ohio suddenly felt like a distant memory, out of step with his reality as an MI officer. "I guess I haven't thought that far ahead. Learning about your experiences got me thinking more about my childhood . . . all the memories." He turned away from Malcolm. "It was difficult to be a Jew in Austria."

Malcolm's mouth tightened. "My parents sent me to a private Catholic school. Our neighbors were like us. I never got close to any Jews. Hadn't ever thought about what it might be like to be persecuted. But I didn't like to be told how to think . . . or what to think." Schlick fell silent, and several moments passed. "It was more about what was ethical. I was uncomfortable belittling any group—Jews, Gypsies, whoever was different. I never really considered how they . . . how someone like you might feel. And I saw no way to fight it." He nodded his head as if affirming this disclosure before he continued. "If I have a future, I want to live in a better world."

Malcolm's words rose into the space like smoke, lifting but lingering as Eli hung onto the boy's hopes. "Turns out we were both persecuted, weren't we?" Eli looked expectantly at Malcolm as he searched for a way to express his aspirations. "I want to get back to Ohio and my new life there. You know, when I lived in Vienna, I skied slopes west of Salzburg. They were beautiful. But that was when I lived in a different world. After this war ends, I may never come back to Austria or Germany." He'd never said this aloud before, had never thought this way until that moment. "And I will finally search out and meet the generous businessman who gave me my freedom."

He turned toward the room's tiny window as their silence was broken by the sound of steps—close, then moving farther away, softening into tranquil background noises. Voices, too, with muted tones of admonishments and appeals to hurry up, mingling like the din of childhood. Above it all arose a gravelly humming—sober and restrained—to the tune "When the Saints Go Marching In."

Eli stood and walked to the window, lifting it up, the cold air seeping inside. He motioned Malcolm to come look. It was pitch-black outside but for the whirls of snowflakes descending, filling the crevices of the hard earth. A white sheen blanketed the Army quarters, transforming it into the villa of its past. Stars flickered through the clouds, their glimmer brief, transient.

The hollow whoosh of wintry wind dissipated into darkness. Eli felt very small and alone. The war stood between him and his family. Between him and his dreams.

Malcolm Schlick, in custody, was now safe.

Part Three

MEETING JOHN BRANDEIS

November 1946

ELI STILL CLEARLY REMEMBERED the first time he heard the name that would come to obsess him—John Brandeis. They'd arrived at Ellis Island, the redolence of the sea still heavy in the air despite the sweaty odor of the hundreds of immigrants disembarking shoulder to shoulder and filling the building where they were eventually examined and questioned. Afterward, they were whisked back to gather their belongings in the grand hall, where a wild scene ensued. Everyone seemed to be shouting at once, hugging one another just like his parents did with Mama's childhood friend, Zelda Muni, patiently waiting to greet them at the end of their journey to America.

It was Zelda who had identified Brandeis as the one responsible for their exodus. With everything swirling around them, Eli had only half heard the name, or maybe he heard it but just didn't dwell on it. Zelda was the one who reached out to Brandeis, but it was Brandeis who actually got them the affidavits. Eli had just been a teenager, eight years and a lifetime ago, and he didn't consider then how these things worked—didn't know it took a person of financial means to sponsor immigrants. The older he got, the more he realized how lucky he was: he had his parents with him, they were safe, they had opportunities and a future. His gratitude morphed into an infatuation with a man he didn't know, a man who became his North Star. Who was this John Brandeis? Why did he help people he didn't know? What made him tick? When Eli returned from the war, he was determined to find a way to meet the object of his obsession.

Eli wanted to learn more about Brandeis beyond the outward facts of his success as a leading business executive and prominent New York retailer. He started in libraries, digging for whatever he could find. He wrote to Zelda, who had become like an aunt to him, and peppered her with questions: What did Brandeis look like? How did he dress? What were the exact details of their interaction those eight years earlier? But, after getting all that information, he realized he still needed more. He sought to stand face-to-face with this man, to understand him, to thank him for saving his life.

Uncharacteristically, Eli devised a crafty scheme. He contacted the Hebrew Immigrant Aid Society. Using an alias, he said he was on special assignment for *The Forward* to write a story on Brandeis and Jewish migration from Europe. HIAS explained that a sponsorship application required a good deal of promised support for émigrés, like housing and job leads. They directed him to several sources to learn more about securing affidavits and finally divulged that Brandeis began sponsoring émigrés from Vienna, Berlin, and Munich as early as '36. They encouraged him to talk directly with Brandeis and gave him the specific address at Stern Brothers where a letter would indeed land on his desk.

It didn't take long for Eli to admit to himself how strange

his behavior had become, how it felt distasteful to carry on like this. All he'd wanted was an address to write to a man he viewed as omnipotent. Now he had it.

THE COMMISSIONAIRE OPENED HIS rear door, tipping his top hat and offering his usual, "Another good day, Mr. Brandeis." Stepping from the sedan, Brandeis felt an anticipatory flash of cheerfulness as he approached his store's grand entrance. It was the Wednesday before Thanksgiving, and he looked forward to the next four weeks of unsurpassed sales.

"Thank you, Hugo. Indeed." Brandeis coasted through the revolving doors and strode across the shiny marble lobby, taking in the rows of floor-to-ceiling alabaster columns to his right and left, each pillar enclosing glass cases of merchandise. He slowed to admire the fine jewelry, perfumes, and cosmetics, nodding to the salesclerks he passed, noting with pride their initiative. Melva, sales lead for jewelry, stood in front of her register counting cash on hand as her assistant meticulously repositioned inventory. Another clerk wiped away smudges on display cases containing the finest of perfumes—Lucien Lelong's Tailspin, Indiscrete, and Balalaika—and customer favorites L'Origan, Emeraude, and Parfums Bright Stars. As he resumed his pace toward the elevators, he inhaled the store's vibrant energy as he would these delicate fragrances.

When the tall brass doors opened, he stepped inside and pressed "B." He entered his executive suite, delighting as he often did in its tasteful elegance. Evelyn was there to take his hat and wool overcoat. He noticed her eyes lingering on the flashy burgundy pocket square he had chosen this morning to play up his otherwise classic gray tweed suit, knowing it was a bit out of character. But he had his reasons.

"Good Morning, Mr. Brandeis. I'll get your coffee and come in to review your appointments." She quickly hung up his coat and disappeared down the hall past her desk.

He peeked over the polished mahogany surface at the calendar book, trying to make out the appointments. He had the desk custom-made earlier in the year to match the suite's grandfather clock. When Evelyn returned carrying a steaming cup of coffee, she swooped up the datebook in her free hand. "No need to read upside down. It'll take but a few minutes to go over your day, Mr. Brandeis." He followed her as she stepped inside his wood-paneled office.

Tomorrow was Macy's Thanksgiving Day Parade, and word spread that it was to be televised by Channel 2—a first. Brandeis was aggravated that Stern Brothers hadn't come up with this kind of promotion. All those marketing people on his staff and not a one had envisioned a creative way to connect Stern Brothers with a high-visibility event like a yearly parade. And why hadn't *he* thought of it? Now, beyond the throngs in the streets, everyone throughout the New York City area owning a television set would be tuning in to learn about all of Macy's upcoming Christmas sales.

"Your first appointment is at ten with David Schuster." Brandeis, listening with one ear, wished he had a window to gaze through while he sorted out life's mysteries. The streaming light might trigger ideas as he watched the bustle of this glorious city. Evelyn's voice kept bringing him back. He heard snippets: about reviewing payroll expenses and needing extra staffing for the holidays, that his buyer for fine jewelry wanted to discuss new promotions. "Your tailor will be in after your lunch with an Eli Stoff—that's the man you asked me to put on today's calendar."

Brandeis perked up, absentmindedly fingering his handkerchief. He looked at his watch. He had thirty minutes before his first appointment. "Thank you, Evelyn. We can review the afternoon schedule while Boris is fitting me for some new suits. Tell him not to come before two o'clock."

After she closed the door behind her, he opened his desk drawer, where he'd kept Stoff's letter. He was dumbfounded when he'd received it and reread it several times to absorb everything the young man had shared. A range of emotions stirred inside him once again, taking him back to that memorable spring day when he met Zelda Muni.

He remembered Mrs. Muni's determination in seeking him out and her assertiveness with his former secretary, who tried to block her entry. Muni carefully introduced herself and her reason for calling on him. An issue of urgency, she had said. A life-and-death matter. Only now did he realize how accurate that plea had been. Muni's impassioned story about her Jewish childhood friend deeply touched him. But the story—about a woman who sought to escape from Vienna at the time of the *Anschluss* with her husband and son—was one he'd heard from so many others: Jews needing a sponsor to get out of Eastern Europe, where anti-Semitism seemed to be backed by a growing political movement. These were the Jews who could see what was coming, although he had not been so prescient. Zelda Muni turned three faceless strangers into people much like his Austrian ancestors. Here was a Catholic woman—an overqualified art historian working as a Waldorf chambermaid to get by in America—trying to save a Jewish family. And identifying him as the one to help make that happen.

For him, it meant financially vouching for Lila and Bart Stoff and their son, Eli, if they became a burden, if they hit hard times. He was in a fortunate position to do so—the son of Jewish immigrants who decades ago built a family-owned department store in Omaha that became the biggest in the Midwest. He knew his was the luck born of circumstance: an upbringing that afforded him a fine business education at the University of Chicago, where he met Irving Stern; then a fix-up with Irv's sister, Eleanor; then the merging of both the families and the businesses. How blessed he was with his two sons and a Manhattan retail empire that stood steady through the Depression.

When Zelda Muni hustled her way into his office, he'd no idea of her purpose. Now, with this imminent visit, Brandeis wondered what had happened to her in the years since their fateful meeting. More fervently, he sought all that lay between the lines of Eli's letter.

October 14, 1946

Dear Mr. Brandeis,

I first heard your name when my family arrived at Ellis Island at the end of August 1938. I thought my mother's childhood friend, Zelda Muni, who greeted us that eventful day, had been responsible for our journey to freedom. My mother explained Zelda's role in our escape, but that you—someone who never knew us and who expected nothing in return—signed our affidavits. Your gift was an act of pure altruism and generosity that I will never forget for the rest of my life.

During our early months, we lived in a cramped apartment in the Lower East Side. I had asked my mother if we could meet you back then so I could thank you. She discouraged me from that, and I can understand how she felt it might be inappropriate for a family of immigrants to suddenly appear at your midtown office. As a fifteen-year-old, I certainly hadn't thought that through.

In the years since—having moved to Columbus, Ohio, finishing high school there, attending Ohio State until I was drafted like everyone else my age, then spending the latter years of the war overseas in military intelligence—I've gained a deep appreciation for what you have done for me and for my family. Beyond giving us an opportunity, you have given us life itself. I have thought about you often.

I will be in New York staying with the Munis over Thanksgiving and would like nothing more than to thank you in person. I will understand if you feel this is unseemly or if the timing is inconvenient. At least I have expressed my gratitude in this letter. I wanted you to know how significant your assistance was for me.

If a meeting is possible, please address a return letter to 1652 Bryden Road, Columbus, Ohio.

In appreciation,
Eli Stoff

Brandeis folded the letter, inserted it back into its envelope, and returned it to his top drawer. Leaning back in his chair, he shut his eyes for a moment, thinking how often one has no idea of the impact one's actions have on another. A request is made. The patron listens and considers and chooses to act, or not. And that decision begets other actions and consequences that ripple like waves in a vast, unseen ocean.

After he heard Madeleine Sheine's proposed one-time holiday discount promotion for Stern's fine jewelry and reviewed her budget for ads—only running the week before Christmas—Brandeis couldn't help checking his pocket watch. Seeing it was ten minutes until noon, he let Madeleine know he'd get back to her on the plan by day's end. As he walked her to the door and wished her a Happy Thanksgiving, he spotted a dark-haired young man sitting in the reception area, turning the pages of a magazine.

Evelyn scurried over, nodding toward the visitor and whispering, "That's Eli Stoff. He arrived early."

∞∞O

Eli's brisk walk to Stern's from the Forty-Second Street and Bryant Park exit settled him down temporarily. He'd left Zelda's Lower East Side apartment a full hour before his noon appointment, glad he had the place to himself that morning, unduly suffused with nervous excitement. When he received Brandeis's reply to his letter three weeks ago, setting an actual date and time for their meeting, he broke into a cold sweat. He'd held inside all that built-up anticipation of someone who was not yet an actual person, but a symbol, a hero. The letter began to make Brandeis real.

As he walked through the revolving doors of Stern Brothers with half an hour to spare, Eli felt his jitters return. He took several deep breaths, slowed his pace, and began to observe his surroundings. The store was elegant, all the marble and brass a step above the one department store in downtown Columbus, Lazarus, that he'd visited only occasionally with his mother. He stopped at the perfume counter and picked a bottle of Skylark eau de cologne he knew his mother would like, then proceeded to the back elevators, where a white-gloved doorman had directed him and pushed "B" for the executive offices. He introduced himself to a redheaded middle-aged woman sitting behind a mahogany desk who kindly greeted him, took his coat, and invited him to wait in the reception area. He tried to look normal and casual as he sat on a cushioned brown couch, picking up a magazine and leafing through it but not really seeing the words or even the photos.

His trance was broken by the sounds of a door opening and the secretary's hushed voice. He could also hear his own heart pumping rapidly as he realized he was about to meet the man who'd consumed his imagination for eight years. And when he looked up, there stood John Brandeis.

Eli caught the genuine affection in Brandeis's eyes even as he took in the man in his entirety: tall and dignified, but also approachable, familiar. Of course, Zelda had described Brandeis in detail all the times Eli badgered her with his questions. And yet it was more than that—not just a familiarity but a resemblance between them. Brandeis could pass as Eli's father more than Eli's own dad; Bart Stoff was completely bald, while John Brandeis's full head of hair was dark, like Eli's, except for the tinges of gray at his temples.

Eli watched Brandeis walk toward him as if in slow motion. He fixed on the man's face, beaming as he offered his hand. Eli almost jumped from the couch like he had awakened from a dream. "Mr. Brandeis! I've looked so forward to this day!"

Brandeis clasped Eli's hand with both of his, then pulled him into a bear hug. "I'm glad you reached out and found me."

Now, the man seemed to be a kindred figure, like a long-lost friend. Caught in a fatherly embrace, Eli was too choked up to respond.

"Eli, have you met Evelyn?" Brandeis turned toward his assistant. Eli nodded meekly. "Evelyn, please get our coats so I can take this young man to a proper lunch."

It was then that Eli noticed the burgundy silk against Brandeis's gray suit. The color combination had to be a coincidence. How would a New York businessman know Ohio State's school colors were scarlet and gray?

Brandeis's black sedan was waiting in front. Eli tried to hide his wonder as Brandeis motioned him toward the back seat. "This is my driver, Victor. Vic, meet Mr. Stoff, and then head west to Sardi's."

After Eli eased himself onto the smooth leather cushion, he felt himself moving forward as if his very life were undergoing a change in this moment. He couldn't take his eyes off the people on the sidewalks. The midtown streets teemed with sophisticated, well-dressed men and women that he hadn't noticed during his earlier walk from the subway: the men in gray-felted fedoras, newspapers bulging from their attachés; women in tailored topcoats, their chiffon scarves fluttering in the autumn breeze. Their quickened steps and intent expressions exposed a dogged pursuit. But of what? Were any of them immigrants like him, working toward an education and a career, perhaps in advertising or law? As the limo sped up, the outside scene flashed past, the people becoming a blur, faceless. He thought about the time he took his mother on a walking tour around Times Square just weeks after they arrived at Ellis Island—all the new sights and the hustle on the streets that excited him as a teenager. But now, he identified with this civilized crowd, just blocks away, not the tourists and workers filling those other sidewalks.

He pulled his gaze back to Brandeis. "I'm sorry I'm so distracted, but—"

"No apologies necessary, Eli. I would assume you haven't been back to New York since '38?"

"We left in early November of that year."

"Well, I'm looking forward to hearing all about the years since then."

∞∞

AT SARDI'S, THE MAÎTRE D' showed them to a banquette. The tables were mostly packed with the typical business crowd and a few diners with the dumbstruck look of tourists.

"We can both sit facing out to see all the goings-on," Brandeis told Eli. "And there will be plenty." The host pulled out the white-clothed table, and they lowered themselves onto the burgundy leather. Brandeis placed the napkin on his lap, watching Eli twist his head toward the rows of images on the upper walls. "The story goes that Vincent, the owner, hired a Russian refugee to draw caricatures of Broadway celebrities in exchange for a meal."

"*Little Lady of Broadway* was playing when I lived here." Eli continued to scan the montage. "Yes! There's the picture of Shirley Temple!"

Brandeis pointed to two pictures in the lower row. "See Alfred Drake and Celeste Holm? *Oklahoma!* has been wildly successful." He searched the wall looking for others. "And the first lady of musical comedy, Ethel Merman. In *Annie Get Your Gun.*"

A tuxedoed waiter came over to take their drink orders and recite the specials. Brandeis studied the champagne list, lingered over the menu. He wanted the lunch to be special for Eli and ordered for both of them: a Dom Pérignon Brut Rosé, a smoked salmon appetizer, and the grilled sirloin. "Enough of these celebrities. Tell me about Zelda Muni."

The waiter placed a basket of bread on the table. Brandeis reached for it, feeling the steam rising as he pulled apart the loaf.

Eli shared the good news that Zelda was working in a small downtown gallery. That Giorgio was finally using his structural engineering skills, thanks to a customer he befriended at his old restaurant. Observing Eli as he spoke, Brandeis was surprised by the young man's comportment. He figured Eli for about twenty-three, but he seemed completely comfortable in his own skin, a trait that many much older lacked. And Brandeis realized Eli spoke with only a slight accent, different from the other immigrants he'd met.

"They have a son who's seven. Umberto. A cute boy."

Brandeis smiled. He remembered Zelda's plea to him years back, how she challenged him to sponsor the Stoffs. He never forgot her exact words: *You have that power. I am just an immigrant chambermaid.* Yet she had found him; she persisted. She was the one who saved this family. When he told her she had more power than she gave herself credit for, he meant it. So he was glad she'd pulled free from her own mental captivity. As Brandeis relived this memory, it seemed to him all the more inconceivable that he sat here with Eli, now a young man, the two brought back to that pivotal moment.

"Aunt Zelda had told me every detail about her quest to find you, about the meeting you had with her." The waiter placed a plate of smoked salmon in front of him. Eli looked up and thanked the waiter, pausing until Brandeis was also served. "She even described your office. I expected to see an unfriendly receptionist—Zelda didn't like your secretary."

Brandeis chuckled. "I've made some staff changes since then."

The waiter set down a silver bucket, the throat of the champagne bottle tilted against one side. Brandeis took pleasure in watching the man ease out the cork with a soft pop, then tip the fizzling pink liquid into their two glasses. His attention shifted to Eli who, open-mouthed, was watching the bubbles rise to the rim, almost overflowing, then settling; he felt Eli's sense of pure wonder.

"Zelda reminded me last night that you were originally from Omaha. It made me think about a man from Omaha I learned about, a Father Edward Flanagan, who built a home for underprivileged boys. He reminded me of you."

Brandeis flushed with pride at the comment, well aware of Father Flanagan's reputation. "That's a generous comparison. How do you know of the priest's good work?"

"When I moved to Columbus, I spent my free time going to American movies so I could speak better English." Eli took a large gulp of champagne. Brandeis smiled at Eli's reaction after he swallowed—raised eyebrows, widened eyes—remembering his first taste of the effervescent drink, how his mouth exploded with flavor.

Eli wiped his mouth with the napkin before continuing. "One of my favorites was *Boys Town*, with Spencer Tracy playing the priest." Eli turned again toward the wall of framed pictures, sweeping his eyes across the rows, then pointing. "See, there's Tracy up at the top. He must have been on Broadway before he went out to Hollywood."

Brandeis liked Eli's passion for movies and his zeal for American cultural icons. That was what he noticed most, beyond Eli's lack of a heavy accent. The boy had assimilated into American culture. He wondered if it was due to living in the Midwest, having served in the Army, or both.

When the steaks arrived, the young man was clearly mesmerized by the table presentation; Brandeis saw how Eli took everything in. Dark brown eyes, like his own, that were discerning, intelligent. A cleft in his chin that gave his face strength. He determined that Eli had never eaten at a place quite this fancy and was happy they came. Eli swallowed his first bite of sirloin. "This is absolutely delicious." He cut another piece. "Do you lunch at places like this every day?"

"Actually, Lenny—my wife—often packs me a lunch and I eat in the office. This—" he gestured with his hand, "is for special occasions." He lifted the bottle from the bucket and poured more champagne in both their glasses.

"I've never met anyone as . . . as important as you are." It was the first time Eli showed any self-consciousness. "But you have been very kind to me and easy to talk with."

"I appreciate that." Brandeis realized how unusual this encounter had to be for Eli, but it was an unprecedented event for him also. "You know, I've never met any people I helped with their immigration. Never got to ask them about their experiences. I've been curious about your transition here. Was it difficult to leave Vienna?"

"I'll give you the short answer. Things in Vienna were demeaning for me—dangerous for all of us—so we were happy to escape. But it was tough to say goodbye to my grandmother."

This was the first Brandeis had heard of another relative. "Mrs. Muni only asked for three affidavits. Did your grandmother get out of the country later?"

"Aunt Zelda didn't know about Gramma Jenny. She was too disabled to travel at that time anyway. My mother kept thinking we'd find a way to get her out once we were settled. By the next year, we lost contact with her." At that, Eli looked away, collecting himself. "We assumed she and my aunt Miriam were sent to the camps like so many—"

Brandeis didn't respond at first. Inside he seethed at the injustice of it, angry at himself for not asking Zelda if there were others. Of course there were others. There always were. He had just accepted her request at face value.

It reminded him of his own more distant past. His *Zayde* and *Bubbe* were Russian Jews who fled pogroms and settled in Vienna. Anti-Semitic policies there drove his parents out. The sacrifice of others allowed him to grow up in Nebraska, to be where he sat today. His thoughts drifted back to the boy and his family, who endured much of the same.

"Your *Bubbe*, after the war. Did your family try to find her?"

∞∞∞

WHENEVER ELI THOUGHT OF his grandmother, he remembered the photograph. In their tiny quarters on the ship they boarded from Trieste, the framed picture fell to the floor, jostled by the boat's movement, and he'd accidently stepped on it, cracking the glass. His mother assured him that the photo was all that mattered, and she'd displayed his grandmother's image prominently wherever they lived, the crack reaching diagonally from top to bottom. He never understood why his mother didn't replace the glass.

He was uncomfortable talking about this raw part of his family history. The truth was that their correspondence with Gramma Jenny ended after 1939. He'd tried to track what might have happened to her during his enlistment, and it led to the same speculative conclusions the family deduced years earlier. His mother took it hard. First there was the guilt about abandoning Gramma, then the grief of her loss. The initial separation, then an absence of communication from Vienna, then not knowing what happened—it all deepened his mother's anguish. Eli felt it like a thick cloud hanging over them.

"What we know is that our neighborhood in Vienna's sixteenth district was bombed in '39. Destroyed. Correspondence with my grandmother ended then, like it did with everyone we knew who couldn't get out. We don't know where the letters we wrote landed, and we received none in return. But it became widely understood that all Jews in the city were removed and sent to camps. So we know she didn't survive. We just don't know the exact details. Better that we don't."

Brandeis finished off his champagne and handed the flute to the waiter. He turned to Eli. "Tell me about that move to Columbus. You were fifteen. That must have been difficult.

Arriving in a new country and then going to a small town where there were few immigrants. In your letter, you said you attended high school and college there."

Eli appreciated Brandeis changing the subject. Now was his chance to share what Brandeis had asked in his letter setting up their visit. "I want to know more about your life," he'd written.

Eli explained the reasons for Columbus—to assimilate, to be near a university, to live in a small community. He told him about his friendship with Hershel Goldstein. "Hershel helped me transition to the public high school. He's who I went to the movies with, and I could ask him anything. It was how I learned about America."

"I guess you could say Hershel became your mentor." Brandeis smiled. "I had a similar friendship with my brother-in-law who is also my business partner. Those relationships are very important. Where is Hershel now?"

"He lives in Chicago. Married a girl from there he met during college." Eli looked down at his empty plate. He felt hollow just then. He hadn't seen Hershel since he left Ohio State in '43 and joined the Army. While they kept in touch, it wasn't the same. "Hershel registered for the draft but flunked the physical. He got a 4-F for flat feet so was able to stay in school."

The waiter brought dessert menus and tidied the table. Brandeis ordered two pieces of cherry pie.

"What about you? When were you drafted?"

Eli described his military experience, from the Mountain Division to Military Intelligence, from Maryland to Manchester to Paris. His role in Alsace analyzing the captured papers on the German V-2 rocket. How his regiment took over Heidelberg. "When the Germans surrendered in April of '45, many of us went to Wiesbaden to assist the new government being set up. We separated the Nazis from those who weren't active soldiers, so you didn't get the same people in power again."

Brandeis, who'd listened carefully, now leaned forward, locking eyes with Eli. "I'm amazed, Eli. Look what you and others like you have done for this country. I feel I'm indebted to you, not the opposite."

"But I owe you my life, Mr. Brandeis, as do so many others. Aunt Zelda told me you helped many Jews escape Europe." He didn't want to add that he also learned about this through his crafty contact with HIAS.

Brandeis helped himself to a bite of the pie the waiter had set down in front of them. "In the first year or two I promised specific jobs or financial assistance—both possible because of my good fortune and the availability of entry-level jobs at Stern's. For a few I found living quarters or provided money to buy food and other necessities. When the Jewish agencies got more involved, my sponsorship focused on the financial only—ensuring the new family would not become a public burden."

Eli thought Brandeis was downplaying his role. "But your deed saved people's lives. It saved my life and that of my parents. I wouldn't be here if not for you!" As other diners turned to look at them, Eli felt himself blush. He realized his last comment had been a loud outburst. But he wanted Brandeis to grasp the magnitude of his help, and Eli's personal gratitude.

"We are not dissimilar, Eli. You've already given back enormously. You risked your life for all of us." He leaned back and took in a deep breath. "The need of Jewish families to leave Europe drew the attention of American Jews like me who could afford to help. It was the right thing to do. That's all."

Brandeis's humility was striking, as was the fact that he saw his enormous deeds as a responsibility. Something expected of him and anyone like him. Eli turned this over in his mind.

"Tell me what you are doing now, Eli."

"Finishing college on the GI Bill. I should have my degree by the end of next year."

"What are you studying?"

"Business. And then I want to go to law school." Eli stared at his hands, clasped on the white cloth in front of him, before he looked up to finish his answer. "Most importantly, I want to give back as you have done, whatever that looks like."

Hearing his own words gave Eli a sudden flash of understanding. *You become. And you are.* John Brandeis's outward success came from a lifetime of hard work and tough choices. But through it all, he never forgot where he came from.

No longer an obsession, or a larger-than-life figure for Eli, John Brandeis was now real. As Eli leaned back against the smooth leather banquette, he looked with affection at the man sitting next to him. A prominent businessman and humanitarian. A first-generation American, the son and grandson of immigrants who fled Europe as Eli and his parents had. A responsible and humble man. And the kind of person Eli wanted to emulate.

TASA'S CHOICE

September 1947

===

TASA WAS BARELY TWO lines into the piece when she heard the front door slam and the excited voice of her mother. Violin in hand, she ran down the steps from her bedroom to find Aunt Norah and Uncle Levi, who she'd not seen for almost a decade. She remembered that hot, humid day at her family's estate in eastern Poland as though it were yesterday—one that began with Danik's affectionate taunts in the orchard and ended in a heated debate about Hitler's growing power and the possibility of war. She was only fifteen then. Now, though safe among relatives in America, she felt herself tense as her father's denial of an immediate threat and her cousin Albert's warnings came back to her.

"Tasa, Tasa! You are a beautiful young woman now." Tears streamed down Aunt Norah's face as she alternatively embraced Tasa and held her away to admire. "Halina, how she's grown and blossomed."

Levi hugged Halina then reached for Tasa while Norah clasped Halina, the scene reminding Tasa of her recent introduction to square dancing with her cousin at a local club. All the stepping on toes as everyone exchanged partners.

"I've missed you so." Halina moved back to survey her sister and brother-in-law. "You must stay at least through the weekend. Salomon will be back soon . . . we have so much to catch up on."

Tasa observed the two sisters as they stood side by side. Norah was smaller, thinner boned, but looked sturdier than her mother. Halina's black hair was thin and dull, her face already etched with lines, her posture slightly stooped. With her smooth skin, Norah looked more like Halina's daughter than her eight-years-younger sibling. Norah, with Levi, had immigrated to the United States before fighting broke out, while her mother had lived in the midst of battle, then been deported to a Siberian work camp. Tasa still carried angst from their five-year separation.

Now, thanks to Papa's brother, they lived together in a small but comfortable house in Atlantic City. Two months earlier she and her parents had arrived at Ellis Island, warmly greeted by Uncle Walter, Aunt Polona, and her cousins Stella and Caleb. She'd felt like a foreigner around her Americanized relatives. Her uncle had left Poland and settled in New Jersey in '21. It was where he'd met Polona, where Tasa's cousins were born. With a successful parking lot business, Uncle Walter bought and furnished this house for them. He said to consider it a loan and took Papa into his business. Meanwhile, Tasa had stayed close to home, occasionally walking along the famous boardwalk and often playing her violin.

Halina took the small bag from Levi and shooed him toward the family room couch. "I'll bring snacks; you must be famished."

Still holding her violin, Tasa lowered herself next to Levi and Norah. "Mama said you'd come visit and told me a little about where you live. In O-hi-o." She tried to pronounce it correctly. "What's it like there?"

"Well, we live near a large university filled with many people your age." Norah looked toward Levi, nodding for him to say more.

"There are nice opportunities in a city like Columbus." Levi's eyes brightened. "I started an office supply business. A number of immigrants also settled there, and we live among a small Jewish community."

Tasa listened, nodding, recalling her mother telling her they had a four-year-old daughter. "How's Franny? I'd love to meet her."

"She'd probably be happier if she wasn't home with a sitter, but I know she'd love to meet you too. If you came to stay with us—to visit—you could teach her music." Norah motioned toward Tasa's violin. "Play something for us. Play what we heard when we were walking up."

The piece was Tasa's favorite Paganini solo. The "Duetto Amorosa" represented a dialogue between two lovers. Tasa blushed at the thought of performing it for them, although they would have no idea of its meaning. Still, she quickly acquiesced, the music a handy substitute when talking became awkward. She put her violin to her chin and placed her bow against the strings to begin the jaunty and optimistic theme, anticipating the more romantic, more passionate and yearning passage to follow. Tasa's heart still ached over the loss of Danik. This song unleashed her sorrow every time she played it.

The front door opened with her father's resounding "*Hej!*" His figure quickly filled the living room entryway.

"Who do we have here?" Salomon scanned the room, beaming.

Tasa stopped playing, stirred by the excited greetings. She still found it miraculous that they were safe, alive, united in America. That they had family around them: some newer, others from their past. The Rosinskis of New Jersey. Now, the Eisens of Ohio. The Dorfmans—Aunt Sascha, Uncle Jakov, and Tolek, who was now seventeen—so close by in New York City and planning to visit soon.

Despite this good fortune, Tasa felt oddly adrift. She had marked time during the war, her aspirations on hold while so many things spun out of control: with their estate commandeered first by the Soviets and then the Nazis, with her mother in Siberia. And in the midst of it all, falling in love and becoming intimate with Danik, then his joining the war effort. She waited years for the war to end, and when it did, she was left to face Danik's death. It took eighteen months in Vienna until they got their affidavits to come to America. After all this time she wasn't even sure what she sought for her future. She was twenty-four and still waiting to begin her life. She had her parents, her new relatives, her violin and her talent, but all this wasn't enough to fill the hollowness she felt in this strange new land.

∞∞∞

"WHAT PLANS DO YOU have, Tasa?" Levi scooped a second helping of salad onto his plate. "I mean, in terms of furthering your education."

"There aren't very good options for me." Tasa picked at her food and began to move it around her plate, a habit she'd acquired at a young age whenever conversation unsettled her. "The two universities that would have made sense for me to attend are far away—more than one hundred and fifty kilometers—" She furrowed her brows for a few seconds, still having trouble with distance conversions. "Maybe a hundred miles from here?"

"Why don't you come back to Columbus with us?" Norah leaned forward and spoke loud enough to get everyone's attention. "We live close to Ohio State. It's a large public university. You could study anything you want there."

"How large is it?" Tasa found her interest piqued by this new possibility.

"I don't know. Levi, what? Maybe twenty-five thousand students?"

"Twenty-five thousand? That's larger than most cities!" Tasa felt overwhelmed by the thought. "How would I find my way?"

Levi swallowed the piece of meat he'd been chewing, then dabbed his mouth with the napkin. "I have a thought. A nice boy about your age works for me. He's finishing business school there right now on the GI Bill. A decorated member of the U.S. Army. I know Eli would be happy to help you get oriented."

Flustered and at a loss for words, Tasa looked toward her parents. Halina, catching her stare, interjected, "I don't understand what you're saying. For Tasa to come with you to Columbus. To live? To attend school? Then to be chaperoned by some salesclerk in your store who fought in the Army? You aren't serious, are you?"

"The young man is from Vienna. Came here at fifteen. Went to school, worked. Then he was drafted like all the rest. A wonderful young man—"

"And he's Jewish," Norah blurted.

At that, Salomon, feigning a cough, held up his hand. "Let's slow down for a moment. We need to know more about this . . . this opportunity for Tasa."

Tasa was indignant. Clearly, her aunt and uncle had a motive in coming to visit. And it seemed that her parents had to be in on the plan. Pushing her chair away from the table, she stood, pasting a wooden smile on her face. "I must be excused, please." She walked to the living room, picked up her violin, and headed upstairs. She needed time to think. Alone.

She paced across the small space of her bedroom. The situation felt strangely like a distant time in her past—half her lifetime ago—when her parents sent her to the next largest town, Brody, to continue her education. Arrangements were made for her to live with a family friend, Greta Rothstein, and attend a private academy that educated Catholics and Jews. Despite this necessary rite of passage, she'd left in tears, afraid to separate from her parents and grandfather. The only consolation had been joining her beloved older cousin, Danik.

A tapping at her door made her jump. She turned to see her mother's head peeking in. "Tasa, please come downstairs. You're being rude."

"Mama, it seems all of you have made plans for me without consulting me first. I am not a child."

"Of course you aren't. This has happened very fast. I just learned of Norah's visit last week and of her . . . her intentions."

"You *knew* about all this, and your apprehension was just an act?"

Halina sat on the bed and motioned Tasa to sit next to her. "I only know that Columbus offers you more than what you have in Atlantic City. We are thinking of your best interests. Look, here you have no good choices. Not for school. Not for meeting young people your age."

"But Mama, it's as though all of you are marrying me off!"

"No, it's nothing like that. This young man has much in common with you. He has friends. He can help you acclimate to a college life. Levi and Norah live within a Jewish community where there are other immigrants from Eastern Europe." She paused, and her eyes softened. "And you could babysit for your cousin, Franny."

Tasa remained silent. There was something enticing about leaving home for a new place where she could be somewhat on her own. Where she could attend a university. While it also scared her, she knew that meeting young people as she'd begun to do in Vienna could shake the melancholy that often gripped her.

"Let me think about this, Mama."

∞∞

TWO DAYS LATER, THEY packed Levi's purple Buick Century with two small bags containing clothes Tasa thought could last her into the cooler fall weather. The heat and humidity on this early September morning brought to mind her final trip with Danik from Podkamien to Brody just a month before Germany attacked Poland. That trip was peaceful, the road empty, the lushness of the land unfurling before her, with its endless, dense fields of sugar beets, their rosettes of leaves spreading upward. Eight years separated two distinct worlds. In one, a horse-drawn carriage transported Tasa for the short journey from her Polish village to the next larger town. In the other, a modern automobile would carry her more than five hundred miles from New Jersey to Ohio.

Tasa viewed this trip only as a trial, which made the departure easier. She would explore what Columbus had to offer her and give it a month or two. It was as if she had a mental list of expectations this new "home" had to fulfill to make it worth yet another separation from her parents. This time, though, the choice to stay or leave was her own.

After parting hugs, Levi keyed the ignition and they were off. He drove down Albany Avenue and entered U.S. Route 40, the highway that could get someone from east to west coasts. Just two blocks from Atlantic City's boardwalk, the view of the vast ocean that connected to her past would soon disappear. Tasa took in the images racing past her window as Levi accelerated to keep pace with the traffic.

She didn't say much for the first two hours of the ride, occasionally asking Levi what city they were driving through, although his answers didn't mean much to her. While they crossed the Delaware River on a ferry, she munched on carrots and pieces of Swiss cheese her mother had packed for the trip. She saw the first of five state markers at the other side—"Welcome to Delaware"—and began getting curious about her destination.

"When did you get to Columbus, Aunt Norah? And why Columbus?"

Norah said their decision to leave Poland came soon after that final family gathering. "That was the last time I saw my papa, your grandfather. Or Danik." Norah's eyes filled. She rolled down the car window before continuing. She and Levi had escaped through Romania and the Black Sea. They felt New York was too crowded. "I'd heard the same about Los Angeles. Columbus appealed to us because of its size and the accessibility to a public university." Tasa learned that Norah had attended Ohio State before Franny was born. "They have a wonderful fine arts program," she added.

"Franny is so lucky to have been born in this country," Tasa observed as she thought about her own itinerant childhood.

"Those years must have been so difficult for you and your father. Your mother shared quite a bit with me in letters and during our visit, but I had heard about her years in Siberia from others. Horrible . . . dreadful to think of such a life you all had. And the miracle that you found one another after all that."

It seemed so long ago, and yet it had been only two years and some months since Mama's emotional return to Poland. Tasa recalled the moment when she and Papa first learned that

Mama was alive, the elation she had felt. Once reunited, the realization of lost time they had to recover hit her hard. As did all the losses they had to absorb.

Even now, the thought that she had lived through the war, and survived it, felt surreal. She deluded herself then, never considering that any one of them could have perished, especially when Germany took over eastern Poland from the Soviets. Her father's presence instilled her with a false sense of security. She felt protected by Danik as well, his loss even weightier than that of their homeland. *To think that our beloved Podkamien is now part of the Ukraine . . .*

The lull of the car's motion relaxed her. The ebb from conversation transported her into a deep trance until she bolted awake—she'd been running through a field with shots flying overhead. She must have cried out because Levi asked if she was okay. "I'm . . . I'm fine." She took a deep breath and stretched her arms as far as the car interior allowed to shake off the nightmarish memory. "Where are we?"

"Pennsylvania. You've been asleep for hours. We've driven through Maryland. You missed the Washington Monument in Baltimore. And you know the young man who works for me, Eli Stoff? Before Eli was sent overseas, he trained in a military camp near Hagerstown, Maryland, a small city we passed through two hours ago."

Tasa nodded casually. She had little interest in prolonging a conversation about the young man the Eisens seemed so intent for her to meet. The sun continued to descend as they drove farther west. Hours passed as they traveled through Pennsylvania, then briefly through West Virginia. By dinner, she spotted a "Welcome to Ohio" sign. Levi and Norah suggested stopping to eat before their final passage into Columbus.

∞

It was late at night by the time they parked the Buick in front of the Eisens' house on the city's east side. Norah thanked her friend and neighbor, Sonya, who had been staying with Franny, the child now long asleep. Tasa mumbled greetings before she tumbled into bed herself. Despite sleeping most of the day's trip, her exhaustion seemed to come from something more than the late hour or long drive. Someplace much deeper.

She woke to a child's high-pitched pleas, Aunt Norah's continued shushes, and the smell of brewed coffee. A freckled, curly-haired four-year-old in pink pajamas jumped into Tasa's arms as she emerged, yawning, from the room they had given her.

"Mama said you're my cousin, Tasa. I'm Franny!" The animated child nestled her head against Tasa's neck before she squirmed from the embrace and began bringing several toys into the kitchen.

"Franny, you must calm down. Tasa just woke up!" Norah pulled a chair out from the table, and Tasa plopped into it. "Sorry. She's been looking forward to your arrival. Eggs and toast?"

"That sounds wonderful. I didn't know I could be so hungry." Tasa looked over at Franny, the girl now pouting sullenly. "Come here, sweet Franny. I have been so excited to finally meet you. We are going to have much fun together, yes?"

Franny's grin immediately replaced her sulky expression, and she bounced over to Tasa. "Can we go to the park now?"

"Sweet child. Please help Mama and go play with your dolls while Tasa eats her breakfast. We will all go out together soon." Norah scooped her daughter up in her arms and gave her a hug and a kiss before waving her to the family room.

Later that morning, the three walked down the street to the 571 Shop. Franny skipped along holding her hand as Tasa took in the neighborhood—sidewalks throughout, mature trees offering shade, a smattering of gardens with daylilies, manicured lawns, mostly red brick houses that were small but in good condition, all with front porches.

"How did the shop get its name?"

"That's the address. It's at 571 Rich Street. A wealthy Jewish couple from Columbus created the shop. Offered employment to the many female refugees arriving here in the thirties. It's managed by the Hebrew Immigrant Aid Society."

As they slowed behind several others on the walkway to the shop, Tasa noticed that 571 looked like the other brick houses and apartment buildings along the residential street. "What kind of work do the women do?"

"They're expert bakers and seamstresses. People from all over Columbus come here to have their clothes repaired. Some request a new suit or dress. They bring in a special pattern or fabric they like. And the cookies here . . ."

Just inside the door, Tasa inhaled the aroma of buttery pastries, her eyes first settling on a tall metal unit, each shelf covered with trays of freshly baked butter cookies and loaves of braided challah. The bakery took up half the open space, with glass cases displaying the edibles for sale. Customers lined up in front of it, one woman lowering herself so she was eye to eye with a *Sachertorte*. Tasa assumed the door behind this selling area led to prep space and cooking equipment. Several ladies walked in and out of the door just in the minutes Tasa stood mesmerized by the array of delicacies, her eye on a peach *Kuchen*.

Franny asked her mother if she could greet a teenager standing in the back of the line. Perhaps a neighbor or babysitter, Tasa thought. Norah nodded her approval just before she called out a greeting to a pleasant woman wearing a blue apron coming out of the back kitchen.

"Lila, here you are. The shop is swarming with customers today." Norah waved for Lila to come over to them. "Tasa, I want you to meet someone." Lila was about her mother's age, her brown hair in a bun, a thin dusting of flour on her bib, just parts of a flowered dress exposed. "This is Lila Stoff, Tasa. She works here with me. Lila is known for her scrumptious apple strudel, among her other talents." Norah's face lit up as she faced her friend. "Lila, this is Tasa Rosinski, my niece. She'll be living with us for a while."

"Ah, Tasa. I've heard about you. Polish, yes?"

Tasa began blushing, wondering what had been said in advance of her visit. Just beyond Lila, Tasa viewed the other half of the space—the sewing machines sitting on rows of tables and women bent over a myriad of fabrics and clothing items while talking to the person on their right or left. This shop was clearly a central gathering place of Jewish women and no doubt a fair share of gossip.

"Yes, I came from a village in eastern—"

"Mama—sorry to interrupt." A tall, dark-haired young man nodded his apologies to Tasa. She noticed the cleft in his chin. "Hi, I'm Eli."

She smiled and reached out her hand. "Tasa."

And just like that, they were introduced.

He turned toward Norah. "Hello, Mrs. Eisen, I'm sorry to barge in, but I have a quick question for my mother." Eli pivoted to face Lila. "Mama, do you need me to transport more bags of apples? The grocer said my purchase weighed twenty pounds. Is that enough for today? I do have to get back to work."

Tasa noticed a gentleness in his demeanor. The deep timbre of his voice. His slight accent.

"That's fine. Go." Lila gave him a peck on his cheek.

"You should know that Lila introduced me to her son because I was trying to find someone to teach me how to drive." Norah looked up at Eli. "You were a wonderful instructor." Then, to Tasa, she said, "I was so fond of Eli that I told Levi about him. Next thing I knew, Eli was working at the supply store on Saturdays."

"On Saturdays? Uncle Levi is open on Shabbat?" Before Norah had a chance to reply, Tasa turned to Eli. "And you work on *Shabbos*?"

"Yes, we're not religious Jews. We belong to the reform synagogue down the street. We don't follow strict customs."

Several customers excused themselves to get past the four who were standing in the middle of a growing line for the pastries. Franny ran back and put her arms around Tasa's waist.

"Let me get some strudel for you to take home for Franny." Lila walked with resolve toward the door in the back.

Norah and Eli moved to the side of the glass display. "Just one question before you go, Eli. Tasa doesn't drive, and she is interested in possibly enrolling in the university. Might you have time to show her around?"

Still in earshot, Tasa straightened up quickly, her hand firmly on Franny's shoulder. "I . . . I don't want to be a burden. I can take public transportation, Aunt Norah." To Eli, Tasa rolled her eyes so he hopefully knew she had not put her aunt up to this arrangement.

"No burden. What day works for you, Tasa?"

∞∞∞

WHEN THE BELL RANG early Saturday morning, Tasa trotted down the steps to find Levi already opening the door.

"Eli, what brings you here?" Levi turned to Tasa, a surprised look on his face.

"Your wife enlisted me as a driver. That's why I asked for the day off."

Tasa couldn't see Eli's face when he answered because the door was only partially opened. She assumed her new friend's expression was self-assured and imagined him sporting a sly grin. There was something fetching about him, but Tasa offered no opinion in response to her aunt's repeated questions at breakfast. If Eli was her driver, then she was a girl with a purpose. Excited to see the college campus, she hoped to find a few classes she could sit in on just to see if the school was right for her. And she needed to visit Hillel, where she had learned there was a rabbi who could help translate documents from her Vienna schooling.

Saying their goodbyes, Eli and Tasa set off toward the car, Eli slightly ahead. He opened the door for her, she slid in, and before she knew it, he pulled the car out and was turning west onto Broad Street, a boulevard with planted trees that reminded her of the streets in Vienna.

"Where did you get this car? Seems a bit of an extravagance for a starving college student."

Unperturbed, Eli kept his eyes on the road. "I worked in a junkyard fixing engine blocks of Chevrolets to save for college. Did that for two years, including summers. The owner told me he'd give me this jalopy for one month's pay. Let me fix it up with old parts he had on hand. You wouldn't have driven in it the way it looked then."

He turned the wheel right, and she saw the sign: High Street. "This will take us straight into campus." At a stoplight, her eyes lingered on a scar on his forearm. He caught her look and slid his sleeve down to cover it.

"What was that?"

Eli was quiet.

"From the war?"

He nodded.

"My uncle called you a decorated member of the Army. Said you trained at a camp we drove near on our way to Columbus. I was sleeping. In Maryland, I think he said."

"Camp Ritchie. It was a military intelligence training camp."

"What did they train you to do?"

"Analyze documents. Translate. Interrogate prisoners. Stuff like that."

"Sounds important." Tasa took in his profile while trying to discern his temperament. He was direct, polite. Easygoing. And unruffled.

"I suppose it had its value. Understanding German came in handy. That's why I was at Camp Ritchie in the first place."

With a neutral affect, Eli shared that he was drafted in '43 after nearly three years at Ohio State. At first, he had enlisted as a ski patrol in the Colorado Mountain division, he said, but he got sick and missed shipping out to Italy with his peers. Tasa wondered what illness he had but didn't want to ask too many questions. She was also curious about what happened to the group that had left without him. Before she could ask, he told her the delay may have saved his life, since intelligence officers weren't called on to fight at the front lines so much.

"Really, my Austrian background saved me," he added.

"How so?"

"Anyone who understood German was useful to the Allies. Like I said, I did lots of translation."

She hoped he didn't see her blush in embarrassment, silently chastising herself for not paying closer attention to his earlier explanations. Her English comprehension still suffered when she became distracted, and she found herself somewhat flustered in Eli's presence. She turned her head away from him, noticing at once the charming brick houses and novelty shops. As they passed a bookstore and a couple of bars, she couldn't help but remember her first drive through the Vienna neighborhoods with her parents after the war. She'd spotted a pack of young people walking briskly along the streets back then as she did now. Their car slowed in traffic, and she watched two students enter a cozy diner.

"So, when you returned, you went right back to school?"

"On the GI Bill. I'm graduating the end of this school year."

"What was it like when you got here? You were pretty young, yes?"

"Fifteen. I guess I was just happy to be in a place where I could make friends. For the most part, I was welcomed. At school, at the temple youth group. We lived with a family before we were able to rent our own apartment. They had a son my age who introduced me to his friends."

"Was it difficult for you to learn English? You barely have an accent."

"I went to lots of movies. I liked going, but I also liked that I could hear people talk. That helped me learn quickly."

Tasa had so many other things she wanted to ask him, but they'd have to wait. Eli parked the car at the edge of Ohio State's campus, and they got out and began walking. She had to work to keep up with him, his long strides outpacing her short legs. Soon they were upon an expansive grassy area marked by walks going in every direction. Eli told her all the freshman students would gather there later that week for an "orientation." She wasn't sure what this meant. He called the area where they stood "the Oval" and said it would be organized into as many sections as faculty members who showed up. Faculty would be assigned about thirty students each, and they'd take those students to various classrooms in the buildings that surrounded the Oval. When she asked how many students that might be in all, he said more than five thousand. She now could see how this sizable campus could handle that many.

The administration building was closed. Tasa hadn't considered what was open or closed on a Saturday and realized Hillel would be closed as well. It was Shabbat.

"You didn't have much of a religious upbringing in Vienna?"

"No. Many of my parents' friends, and my friends, weren't Jewish. We didn't live in a Jewish area."

Tasa slowed her pace, considering whether to probe further, then decided against doing so. "You lived in the city your whole life?"

"Yes, in District Sixteen."

"What did you do for fun?"

"I liked to ski and went on school trips, skied the Alps. I enjoy music, especially jazz and opera. We went to concerts regularly."

Of course he would love music. Vienna was suffused with it. Tasa's favorite composers came from Vienna or ended up there. "I'm a musician, a violinist. I've played since I was a child."

"Really? I'd love to hear you play." Eli's cheeks flushed with excitement.

It was the first time he exhibited true enthusiasm since he had picked her up. When he smiled, his brown eyes sparkled, and his whole face took on an innocence that appealed to her. She couldn't deny that he was extremely good-looking. That tall, dark, and handsome type. Lean but rugged. "Since everything is closed here and it's getting late, why don't we go back to your aunt's apartment and you can play something for me? And maybe later we should go to a place that has music. Do you like to dance?"

Tasa beamed. "Yes, I love to!"

As they drove from the university, he told her about Valley Dale and its grand ballroom, where big band names like Frank Sinatra and Tommy Dorsey often performed. Tasa forgot that she'd gotten nothing accomplished that day—she hadn't even gotten a course catalog, hadn't gotten her transcripts translated to explore what her credit transfer and thus class placement *could* be—as she was busy answering Eli's questions about her background in Poland. She began to share some of the things that happened during her teenage years under Soviet then German rule, and the year she hid underground with her father and other relatives. She didn't mention Danik. Eli's interest was genuine, his query gentle, and she found him easy to talk to. Distancing herself from the horrific reality of her experience, she spoke as if telling a story about someone else.

∞∞∞

THEY FOUND NO ONE at home. Tasa called out, then peeked her head in the various rooms. As she took her violin from its case and walked to the living room where Eli was patiently sitting, she considered what to play for him. She thought of her last week in Vienna, the prolonged walk she took one Sunday morning before the city awoke, the stroll in Stadtpark that brought her face-to-face with the lifelike statue of Johann Strauss Jr., the Waltz King.

Her choice became clear.

As she set her bow on the strings, the melodic notes conjured images of the wooded eastern foothills of the Alps, the sounds of birds in song, and the flowing water of rivers—the countryside, the Vienna woods. She could hear that distinctive plucking of the zither and imagined the world of peasants dancing wildly at first, their whirling movements and gaiety. Then the graceful waltzing. It was Eli's shouts of "Brava!" that broke her trance.

She placed her violin and bow down, blushing, and quickly asked if he'd like an iced tea. As she went to fetch two glasses in the kitchen, a wave of grief for Danik suddenly rushed to the surface, catching in her throat. This pushed against other feelings, for Eli, undefined just yet. There was so much she chose not to share it choked her heart. She took several deep breaths to tamp down the swirl of emotion before stepping back to the living room.

The two continued to talk about their shared Eastern European roots well into the afternoon. The music had created a bond, a comfortable bridge between her rural, sheltered world and his urban, exposed one. Yet there was a wide gap between their experiences as war approached. After all, in the spring of 1938, Tasa was just finishing lower school with a promising future ahead as a violinist. She lived amid the countryside of eastern Poland in a gorgeous new house outlined by linden trees on land bordered by a lake, among family and friends whose illusory wall of safety was just beginning to show cracks. Eli lived in Hitler's immediate shadow, among men in Nazi uniforms exchanging greetings of *"Heil Hitler!"* He seemed reticent at first to talk about the months and days leading to his family's departure.

"You don't like to talk about it. Why?" she asked him.

"It was the *Anschluss*. I was there. Coming back from a school ski trip. I knew then the futility of a Jew remaining in Austria."

And so Eli began to share what happened to him when he was fifteen, the same age as Tasa when her family argued on a hot, humid day about the possibility of war.

AN IMMIGRANT'S ODYSSEY

January 1948

IT HADN'T BEEN EASY for Arthur Zeidl to locate Lila Stoff. He'd last seen her at her father's funeral, a full year before the Nuremberg Laws would officially have robbed him of his professorship at the University of Vienna. He didn't wait around for that to happen. Not long after that service, he fled to Shanghai. Lila escaped a few months after the Anschluss, immigrating to America and, he learned, settling in Ohio. When he arrived at her home with his life's possessions contained in a single suitcase, he'd only planned a brief visit.

He knew it odd. A middle-aged bachelor living with his first cousin, her husband, and their son in their tidy apartment in a Jewish neighborhood in Columbus. Yet it filled him with a deep contentment he hadn't felt since long before the war. The Stoffs and their tight-knit community welcomed him. This Midwestern town of immigrant neighborhoods made him feel, finally, at home.

Lila had just gone to bed—Bart had turned in even earlier—and Arthur's conversation with her still echoed in his head as he waited up for Eli. He felt even closer to Lila than during their childhood. Beyond the fact of their mothers being twins, this deeper bond came from sharing the uncertainty of not knowing when and how each had died at the hands of Nazis. As he sat with Lila, their cups of steaming tea in hand, so much of their talk kept going backward. It always began with the guilt.

"If only I had asked for more visas." Lila once again admonished herself for her omission—for not specifically requesting a visa for her mother in the desperate letter she wrote to New York, to her childhood friend Zelda Muni. By then, the ports were closing one by one; destinations were growing fewer and fewer by the day for Jews trying to find a way out. Three visas arrived for Lila, Bart, and Eli. Arthur knew how much Lila's oversight plagued her.

"You think your mother would have left Vienna? She was as obstinate as mine," he told her as he recalled his own urgent appeals back then, his mother refusing to leave her sister, her home, or the city she loved.

Arthur shared the wistful effect the loss of his mother still had on him. Lila voiced the same nostalgia, tied to a loss of their Viennese childhoods, of their fathers and grandparents—all gone. She asked him what he remembered about his mother, her aunt Miriam. And Arthur had to chuckle as he blurted without a pause: "Her bad cooking." Lila then described her cherished memory: the afternoon when Eli turned three and she brought along her fancy new camera on their family outing in Stadtpark. Arthur saw her eyes glisten as she spoke of the country's strength—the Great Depression hadn't yet arrived—and how happy they were as a young family. Bart and Eli were frolicking, so Lila decided to practice using the camera on a more stationary subject, her mother. Arthur admired that lovely portrait from where he now sat. It was as if his aunt Jenny were there with them in the living room.

Vienna seemed present, too, as he continued to replay their conversation, which inevitably moved to their much-adored city. He liked remembering the Vienna of their past. All their talking brought that place and time back to life: meeting friends at the sidewalk cafés for *Sachertorte* and Viennese coffee, strolling along the Danube, attending Sunday matinees at the Volksoper for opera or Friday evening open-air concerts in summer, the sounds of violins playing Shubert, Mozart, or Strauss wafting like a gentle breeze. Lila shared her delight in going to Prater, the amusement park, and riding the *Reisenrad*, but Ferris wheel rides weren't Arthur's favorite pastime. He loved the snowy hills of Vienna and the Austrian winters. And best were the times their families sat around telling stories late into the night, as he and Lila had done this evening.

Arthur's immediate family, like Lila's, was secular, assimilated. They were Austrians first, Jews second. But the economic malaise and political unrest of the '30s changed that allegiance for him. Anti-Semitic slogans were smeared on shop windows he used to visit as a child. He began to hear rumblings at the university that he found insulting and incriminating: falsehoods and accusations about Jews and their role in Austria's financial demise. What did religious views have to do with a country's fiscal trajectory? The university—like the country itself—used to be civil, not vindictive and punitive. He felt this increasing animosity even from non-Jewish friends. With each Nazi salute of *Heil Hitler* he witnessed, Arthur grew more agitated, felt more threatened. The last straw was when Lila told him of her visit to her father's gravesite, the cemetery desecrated and vandalized, with headstones throughout the Jewish section overturned, swastikas painted everywhere. In quiet desperation, he began searching for a safe haven. But it was hard to get passports, and he learned that many countries strictly capped immigration.

When he first heard Shanghai whispered in the streets, it sounded exotic and remote and he sought details, trying to understand why this city might offer a refuge. Visas and police certificates weren't required; passport inspection didn't greet émigrés upon arrival there. The Chinese didn't even expect proof of financial stability as so many other countries demanded. Arthur relayed all this to his mother, but she thought him foolhardy. Lila and her family were too shaken over her father's death then to make any decision. He had nothing keeping him in Austria, so he finally moved ahead with his plans alone, despite his misgivings at leaving his homeland and loved ones.

At the emigration office, he found long queues and gruff uniformed men shooting barbs at the Jews. He was told to sign an affidavit that would remove his rights as an Austrian, marking him as a displaced person. His passport was stamped with a *J*—and he realized secular Austrians like himself were lumped together with the religious Jews, all by a single letter. As he recounted this story to Lila, he told her: "We all had become outsiders in our own country."

"At least we never had to watch the synagogues burn and the streets fill with shattered glass," Lila reminded him. True, he hadn't experienced that horror. He'd been living in Shanghai for nearly a year when he caught the news about *Kristallnacht*. "Our beloved Vienna. What a ravaged mess it became," she said with a sigh. "All its civility and finery slaughtered along with our people."

∞∞

THE CUCKOO BROKE ARTHUR'S reverie. Ten o'clock. He rubbed a hand across his forehead, Lila's gentle goodnight kiss still freshly imprinted. He stood and stretched, then walked to the kitchen to boil more water for tea. With the January cold seeping into the cozy apartment, he warmed his hands on the cup. Funny how in Shanghai he drank tea all day despite the sweltering heat, or even because of it.

He heard the creak of the porch screen and the shutting of the door and strode back to the living room to find Eli. "I was just making tea. Would you like some?"

"Yes! Please. It's bitter out there." Eli removed and hung up his wool hat and overcoat.

"I had a nice evening with your parents. Your mother and I spent some time reminiscing." Arthur brought out another cup and sat on the couch next to Eli.

Eli put his tea down and leaned back, a wide grin on his face. "It must be the cold weather that just made me think of this, but remember the time you took me skiing? You talked so much about the beauty of Austria's snow-capped mountains—I assumed you were an expert."

"Okay, okay. I'll admit I never was an athlete. But I did adore the scenery." Arthur brought the cup to his lips, sipping, as his mind drifted to the image of his stop-and-start run down the slopes as ten-year-old Eli tried to offer him pointers. "Back then, you were more respectful."

He loved his banter with Eli, an ease that came from being like an uncle, as Eli affectionately called him, even though they were in fact second cousins, an ease not present between Eli and his own father. It wasn't just that Bart was an older father, now sixty—twelve years older than Lila, a decade senior to Arthur—but he was a man more set in his ways, less intellectually curious. It made his transition into American life more difficult—he struggled with the language, the customs, the pace. When Eli and Bart were together, Arthur observed the interaction between an eager, assimilating youth and an old-world immigrant. He sensed a father's love but not a fatherly understanding of what motivated Eli or captured the boy's imagination. Arthur wasn't sure he could really know, either, but he wanted to try.

"I deserve your teasing. You'd become a great skier by the time I left Vienna a few years later. It was just after your *Opa* died and, then, so many changes for all of us. But at least we still have your mother's *Wiener Schnitzel*."

"Thank God for that! Mama keeps Vienna close in her kitchen. Every day."

"Also when we get the chance to hear her play the piano— all those wonderful Mozart concertos." Arthur played piano himself, but rarely when in the Stoffs' presence.

"I love when Mama plays 'Eine kleine Nachmusik.'" Eli grew quiet, as though lost in some thought of his own. Arthur felt no need to fill the silence, broken only by the ticktock of the cuckoo clock. "Do you miss Vienna, Uncle?"

"I carry it with me. Along with all the family and friends who are lost to us." Arthur's thoughts strayed to the hot chocolate and roasted marshmallow he'd order at Demel's pastry shop, where he'd go with his parents on a cold wintry evening like this. And to the summers. "Vienna's music is still in the air I breathe, just like the aroma of the roasted wieners peddled in Stadtpark."

"Why did you go to Shanghai when so many of us were trying to get into America?"

Eli's question caught him off guard. "You know, ships from Vienna went to many ports besides the United States— to Palestine, Australia, Canada, South America. Where we all ended up had to do with timing and getting affidavits." The tea roiled in his stomach, like the sea, with the memory. "It took a month to get there. I wasn't the best traveler in bad weather."

Arthur shared his escape with Eli, including his journey on an

Italian ship that traveled from Genoa some seven thousand miles to Alexandria, through the Suez Canal, sailing along the Red Sea to Bombay to Hong Kong to Shanghai.

"It took us two weeks to get to New York, and that felt like forever." Eli sunk deeper into the couch. "What was it like when you got there? I can't even imagine . . . I mean, where did you live?"

Arthur drew in a deep shuddering breath, trying to retrieve those very visceral impressions he had fresh off the boat. "Taking in the whole scene, that whole chaotic spectacle . . . it was . . . well, it was nothing like the life we had in Vienna, or like anything I'd ever experienced."

He recalled the vertigo of his odyssey. "I arrived in the morning. It was already sweltering. Wobbly rickshaws darted in and out of traffic. The streets were packed. People everywhere. And trolley cars. The odor of garbage and sewage sickening."

Eli's eyes widened. "I know this isn't really any comparison, but when we got to the Lower East Side it was August, and I remember sweating through my clothes. There was a lot of squalor on the streets and a pungent smell. I guess from the mix of all the kosher and Chinese restaurants. A Jewish aid group who met us at Ellis Island found us our temporary apartment there. Where did they put you up?"

Arthur laughed. No one was waiting for him in Shanghai. He and the others were on their own, but they quickly got the lay of the land. He learned about an old church that housed transient refugees. Before long, the nuns who ran the place were trying to convert him and other Jews. He had brought with him a small sum of money and soon applied for an apartment. He got one in "French Town," where other refugees settled. As a single man with few needs, he lived in a small portion of the space—with a cot, a small bathroom, and a kitchenette—and rented out the rest to a young German family for income. Over time, he invested in other apartments and rented them out. That became his income while he volunteered at a nearby school and taught English.

"So, you had to find a new way of getting along on your own. You must have been lonely, Uncle. I had to find my way, but I had my parents." Eli talked about their brief stay in New York and his mother's desire to move to a town where they could assimilate, with a university. "The Jewish agency gave us a list. I chose Columbus because of that Olympic star Jesse Owens. He'd gone to Ohio State and made Hitler look bad."

"Ah, so that's how you ended up here." Arthur had figured the family was assigned to the city. "I wasn't lonely for long. There were so many of us refugees. We stuck together. But enough of all that. Tell me about your plans right now."

Eli spoke about his schoolwork, how he would graduate from Ohio State in June with a business degree, that he didn't know what to do next. His part-time work with Levi Eisen at the supply store could become full-time, but he was thinking about going to law school. "You know, if it wasn't for the GI Bill, I wouldn't have been able to finish college when I came back from the Army. With my degree, I can get into law school. Work days and go to classes at night."

"Sounds like a great plan. Now, tell me about the girl. That's where you were tonight?" Lila had told Arthur about the Polish émigré named Tasa who Eli met last September.

Eli nodded. "She's really nice. Intelligent. Pretty. And she plays the violin beautifully. The Eisens plucked her from her family in Atlantic City two months after they arrived at Ellis Island." He stopped at that.

"It all sounds wonderful. Does she make you happy?"

"Well, yes. I'm really fond of her." Eli squirmed a bit on the couch and stood up to stretch. "Can I take your teacup to the kitchen?"

Arthur handed his cup to Eli, thanking him. He sensed Eli had more on his mind but decided to let him take the lead.

Eli returned with a plate of Viennese fingers. "Another treat from the homeland. Mama used to make these all the time for my friends when we first got to Columbus. I was pretty popular." He grinned broadly before he dropped back onto the couch. The munching of butter cookies replaced conversation.

"It might have been even better with a fresh cup of tea." Arthur wiped his mouth with his napkin.

Eli pushed the plate away after popping the last cookie in his mouth. "So where did I leave off? Oh, yeah, Tasa." He paused. "I like her a lot. But I worry about our differences. I mean, well, we both have Eastern European roots, but she's literally just off the boat—"

"Might I remind you that you were just off the boat as well at one point." Arthur offered his message with a twinkle in his eye.

"You're right. Absolutely right. It's just that Tasa grew up really sheltered. I mean, she lived in a rural enclave in some tiny Polish village until she left for a nearby private school. Closely cared for there by a family friend. Even when the war broke out and she had to live in hiding, it seems like her father shielded her."

"So, you think this different experience is something that would cause . . . some discord between you?"

"I'm not saying that. It's just that I grew up like you: in a cosmopolitan city. I served in the U.S. Army and saw much of the world in an unprotected way, if you know what I mean."

"It sounds like Tasa saw a bit of the world as well, protected or not. Where did she go after the war?"

"She spent about eighteen months in Vienna waiting for visas from her uncle in Atlantic City."

"Ahhhh." Arthur nodded, as if to himself. "You know, it

sounds like this young lady might have had quite an interesting journey. And, living in Vienna after the war . . . not an easy time to be there." He paused, pensive for a moment. "I look forward to learning more, maybe from her directly. Might you arrange a time for the three of us to get together? I certainly must hear her play the violin."

ARTHUR HAD LOOKED FORWARD to this evening, when he would join Eli and Tasa for dinner downtown. Eli said he'd already taken Tasa to this restaurant, The Tremont. "They have prime steaks broiled to order, free parking, an organist playing show tunes, and—you might want to know this—the best-looking waitresses." Arthur chuckled to himself thinking how Eli tried to entice him, as if their company wasn't enough. He decided not to remind Eli the get-together had been his idea to begin with.

He drove with Eli to pick up Tasa, calling out to him as he walked to the Eisens' front door. "Don't forget. I'd like her to play for us after dinner." He watched their easy repartee as they approached the car, Tasa cradling her violin. He could see how Eli could fall for this pretty young woman—her thick dark hair spilling over her shoulders, her petite stature, the fetching way she smiled up at him, then slipped her free arm into the crook of his. Her greeting to Arthur was equally warm. "I've heard such wonderful stories about you from Eli," she said, clasping his hand in hers, her thick accent making *heard* sound like "hurt" and *wonderful* coming out "vonderful."

As they walked through the door of The Tremont, a few bars from "Almost Like Being in Love" filled the air. Tasa's cheeks grew red and she scurried to the coatroom. Eli spoke in a low voice to Arthur. "I told you about the organist. Name's

Vivian. She has this way of befriending the couples who dine here." He rolled his eyes before continuing. "She took a special liking to us when we came a few weeks ago. Let's just say the *Brigadoon* piece was her way of saying hello to us."

To the strains of "How Are Things in Glocca Morra?" Arthur nodded to Vivian as they were escorted to a red leather wall booth not far from where she stroked the keys of a Hammond organ. His eyes took in the large dining room. The Cape Cod wallpaper with its outline of sailboats cast an American feel, but the recessed neon lighting brought to mind the nightclubs in Shanghai.

"Very festive here." He smiled at the young couple across from him. "It makes me think of a dance hall in China. Oddly on the top floor of a department store. Had a big band there performing the Broadway songs of Cole Porter and Irving Berlin."

"I'd love to hear about your time there, Arthur." Tasa's dark eyes intently fixed on his.

"Shanghai's a bustling city—very cosmopolitan. A bit like Vienna, where I understand you spent some time after the war."

"But I didn't go to dance clubs, as much as I might have wanted to. I never would imagine Shanghai as a place filled with such . . . well, I have a vague, but more destitute, picture."

"The city had that side too. But I dated a Jewish émigré from Salzburg named Ana there. She worked as a hostess in a posh nightclub frequented by the city's royalty." Arthur could still smell the aroma of perfume and the foul odor of the streets, two worlds, really—royalty and refugees—living side by side. "Through Ana, I learned about the private clubs—for Americans, British, French, Russians, and Chinese. There was even a German club. They were each an oasis from the misery outside."

"Yes. It was the misery, the poverty, that I imagined."

"Before Japanese troops invaded and took full control, Shanghai had an area called the International Settlement with many nationalities operating self-governing fiefdoms exempt from Chinese law. It was where much of the wealth was concentrated. Until '41, Shanghai was a political anomaly."

Over the meal of brisket and fingerling potatoes, Tasa and Eli kept prodding Arthur with questions. Tasa wondered how many Jews were actually living in Shanghai. The first group consisted of hundreds of wealthy Sephardic Jews who arrived from Iraq as traders in the mid-1800s, Arthur told her. They were powerful icons who owned luxury hotels and other property. Several thousand Russian Jews who fled the Bolshevik Revolution in 1917 made up the second and larger community. In Shanghai, they gained such status that a main street leading from the heart of the city was often called "Moscow Boulevard."

In the late '30s, Shanghai remained the only city open to Jews without sponsors. During the early stages of Nazi rule, the Jewish population grew by tens of thousands. "By the time World War II broke out, I bet more European Jews had taken refuge in Shanghai than in any other city in the world."

"That's incredible. What happened to Ana?"

"She's still there. We eventually grew apart. I wasn't one for commitments, especially since I had no intention of staying there and Ana wanted to integrate into the Chinese culture. Hard to get serious when you have no sense of a future together." As he got the words out, he noticed a wistfulness in Tasa and her veiled glimpse at Eli.

After they ordered banana cream pie for dessert—encouraged by the waitress to try the house special—Arthur sat back to enjoy Vivian's voice and the melody she was singing. Her lyrics portrayed a "bright golden haze on the meadow" and corn "as high as an elephant's eye" that was "climbin' clear up to the sky." It *was* a beautiful day, he thought. A beautiful life now that war was past.

When they returned to the Stoffs', the house was dark, Lila and Bart out with friends for their weekly canasta game. Eli hung up their coats as Arthur hurried to the kitchen to prepare some tea. Tasa had already taken her violin out when he returned to the living room and was admiring several wood carvings propped along the fireplace mantel—one of a deer, another of flowers—as Eli talked about his mother's fondness for art, mentioning the classes she often took in sculpture and painting.

"That's what I love about Columbus," Tasa was telling Eli as Arthur set down the tray, the heat of the tea steaming upward. "It's small enough to easily get around, yet there's so much here—the arts and culture, access to a great public university, a close immigrant community."

"Yes. This vibrant community is what appealed to me," Arthur chimed in. "It was something that slowly developed in Shanghai as well. When you were in Vienna, did you find a tight circle of Jews there?"

"I . . . I stuck pretty close to our apartment in the American district the first few months. I was still shaken by personal losses, just coming out of war. But I began to feel part of the city, started attending school." Tasa gestured to her violin. "Music helped me get through so much."

"Let's hear a bit." Arthur sensed that Tasa didn't want to talk further about her experience. He settled back into the couch next to Eli as she picked up her violin and drew out a few notes, testing and adjusting. Satisfied, she held the instrument to her chin and began with an upward stroke of her bow, unleashing a melody that conjured for him images of peasants living in the forested playground of the Vienna Woods. As her clear and high-pitched twangs, gentle at first, began moving faster, Arthur visualized the peasants' gaiety and whirling movements, the very folkish scene blurring into a familiar waltz narrative of city life. He let the music enter his entire being, transporting him to his homeland, his past, to his younger self dancing, the triple time guiding him and his partner as they spun rhythmically around and around the floor's edges. So immersed was he in the music that he was jolted, as if from a dream, when Tasa played her final note.

"BRAVA!" Arthur rose from the couch, clapping, as did Eli. Tasa took a bow, a blush fanning across her neck as she carefully placed her bow and violin down and eased herself next to Eli.

"Your playing reminds me of a young Viennese violinist I befriended in a coffee shop in Shanghai." Arthur had heard the young man playing outside and was impressed with his talent. It was a dreary day, and when raindrops turned into a downpour, he invited the musician to join him for coffee. "To repay me, he invited me to hear his small concert in a dingy hall in the Little Vienna section of the Shanghai ghetto."

Eli sat forward on the couch. "There was a ghetto in Shanghai?"

"Not at first. It formed as Japanese troops invaded Shanghai's international settlements and took full control of the city after Pearl Harbor. Japan's German allies pressured them to contain the Jews, so they ordered all DPs into this impoverished one-square-mile area. By the spring of '43, there could have been twenty thousand of us."

"Like the Warsaw Ghetto?" Tasa's brows fretted together.

Arthur saw how each of their perspectives on the war came from where they were located: Eli in the U.S., where much information had been suppressed, and Tasa in Poland, trying to evade the Nazis. "Somewhat like Warsaw, but not as threatened. I had to move from my apartment in French Town to Hongkew, as it was called. The conditions were far from ideal, but the residents sought to form a community. They opened a bakery, a butcher shop, a Viennese-themed restaurant, a coffee shop. They even established a school for Jewish kids. And that music hall.

"The young violinist played like you, Tasa." As though it were yesterday, Arthur could visualize his young Viennese friend. How his whole body inhabited the music and his entire spirit entered his instrument—his past anguish, the freedom he was beginning to savor, his thirst for survival. "He may have had a different journey, but a common passion. A common spirit. Like all of us."

Arthur glanced over at Tasa and Eli. He saw a glow of pride light up Tasa's pale complexion. And he caught something new in his young cousin. A sense of fulfillment, as though the evening had brought him clarity. In that flash of contentedness and tranquility in Eli's eyes, Arthur could see the promise of their future together.

THE WEDDING

June 11, 1948

ELEANOR POSITIONED HERSELF ON a wooden bench in the synagogue lobby facing the front door. Dressed in a simple linen frock, she had her unruly blond hair pulled into a topknot, her nails painted pink for the occasion. The Rolleiflex rested at her side. Here she could see the people as they entered. Her subjects. Those family and friends described to her by Lila Stoff, the mother of the groom. She heard distant laughter outside. Moments later, a stream of light nearly blinded her as the front door opened. It was a brilliant June day, perfect for a wedding.

Her eyes adjusted quickly to the three men chortling among themselves, clearly happy to be in one another's company. As they nodded to her, she figured them to be Eli's Camp Ritchie friends—the four had trained together to become military intelligence officers before they were sent overseas. They were the lucky ones who returned. She stood eye to eye with them as she introduced herself, her height always making her self-conscious.

Only when she was behind a camera did she melt into the scene and feel completely at ease.

Just last month she received the call from her aunt Emma in Columbus. Emma Goldstein was Eleanor's mother's sister. And Lila Stoff was Emma's best friend. The ladies worked together every day and played canasta in their free time. Their families were close. "Lila's been fretting about pictures of her son's wedding," Emma had explained. "I said I knew the perfect photographer. I told them all about you, and when Lila worried about your having to come down from Cleveland, I said June would be a wonderful time for you to visit our family. Isn't that so, Eleanor?"

The thought of recording a festive affair did seem a welcome break, so Eleanor listened with interest to her aunt's proposition. In the years since she'd taken up her post at the *Cleveland Plain Dealer*, she'd earned seniority and, within reason, could set her own schedule.

She had arrived two days earlier and spent much of her time with Lila, who was in charge of the wedding arrangements because the bride's parents lived in New Jersey. Lila gave her a list of family members and close friends who'd be attending and filled in the details of each person's relationship with the couple. Eleanor asked a lot of questions during their briefing. She knew her keen understanding of each of them would allow her to precisely tell the human story of this wedding day, their precious moment in time.

She felt at ease staying with her aunt Emma and uncle Simon and enjoyed catching up with them and her cousins, whom she hadn't seen for several years. Meyer was now twenty and a junior at Ohio State, and Hershel, Eli's closest childhood friend from Columbus, was married; he drove in from Chicago with his wife, Rebecca. Spending several days in Columbus made this visit feel restful, unhurried. And instead of waking up this morning thinking about which dress to wear (she only brought one) and how to do her hair (get it out of her face), Eleanor's mind focused on the checklist in her head—camera, film, flash bulb, tripod . . .

Now, as she sat alone in silence, she looked forward to connecting faces with the names and backgrounds Lila had given her. Eli entered the synagogue next and immediately joined his friends, striking in a gray double-breasted jacket, with faint white pinstripes running down the length of his cuffed trousers. Lila and Bart Stoff followed behind him, Lila wearing a charcoal suit with a lacy blouse, Bart a tailored suit similar to his son's. Eli excused himself and walked over to his parents. The three murmured among themselves, seemingly unaware of Eleanor's presence. As Lila adjusted the knot of Eli's necktie, Eleanor flashed back to the photograph Lila had shown her of Eli as a toddler playing in a Vienna park. She cleared her throat to get their attention and quickly stood as Lila approached and gave her a hug, introducing her to Bart and Eli.

"I've heard so much about you from your mother." Eleanor offered her hand to Eli. "A regular war hero."

"Nice of you to say, but I was no different than any other GI serving our country." Eli gave her a warm grin, his pronunciation revealing a slight German accent. "Mom tells me you're Emma and Simon's niece. You know we lived with the Goldsteins when we came to Columbus. I'd love to hear old stories about Hershel."

"Of course. I'm sure I can come up with a few you haven't heard before." Eleanor turned to Bart. "You must be proud of your son, sir. And I've enjoyed getting to know your wife."

After pleasantries, the three left Eleanor in the lobby and headed to the chapel. She waited until most everyone arrived, particularly wanting to greet Tasa, who came with her parents,

Halina and Salomon Rosinski. Tasa appeared angelic in her tailored off-white suit, tiny pearl buttons adorning her quarter-sleeve jacket. Her skirt's flowing pleats hung midcalf, showing off high heels. Halina wore a brightly flowered dress, her raven hair parted in the middle like her daughter's, smoothed perfectly into a bun at the nape of her neck. Salomon's suit was a single-breasted charcoal brown, embellished with a stylish blue tie. Their faces expressed a worn happiness—like soldiers returning from battle, anticipating their reunion with loved ones. Eleanor couldn't help admiring Tasa's thick eyebrows, her own so faint and indistinct, and she imagined Tasa often tightening them in concentration or worry, given what her aunt and Lila had told her about the young woman's early life in eastern Poland during wartime. She also took note of Tasa's coal-black eyes, her soft, round chin, her easy smile.

She rose and introduced herself to the Rosinskis. Their voices must have carried into the chapel because the Stoffs returned to the lobby, and there were warm hugs all around. Eleanor had the urge to snap a picture right then. She observed how Eli took in the woman who would be his life's partner. She watched as Tasa rested her arm on his shoulder. As the time drew near, the rabbi ushered the families into the chapel. Salomon tenderly put his hand on his daughter's cheek, then kissed the top of her head.

It reminded Eleanor of her affectionate relationship with her own father, an engineer with an attention to detail and a desire to figure things out. Like him, she was both creative and mechanical, and they shared a love of cameras. When she'd found an old view camera in their attic, he enthusiastically supported her childhood hobby, and by the time she was twelve, she began to hang out at a nearby camera shop and take out books at the library to learn more about what this magical instrument could do. She became the family photographer, taking the usual travel snapshots but also portraits of her parents, her younger brother, her girlfriends. Like her mother, Eleanor noticed everything around her, and the camera's lens revealed even more than her own eye. While she was drawn to realistic photography and ended up a photojournalist, she always felt the urge to experiment, to better learn how to capture the essence of a scene or person. For her, photography was a way to be exposed to unfamiliar situations and people and, through her camera, come to understand them. Sometimes the *Plain Dealer*'s tight deadlines constrained her ability to explore deeply enough, to truly reveal through images. At this wedding, she'd put her heart and mind into the preparation so she could squeeze meaning into every gesture of affection and fellowship through her images.

By now, guests were streaming into the temple lobby, happily mingling. Eleanor decided to stand off in a corner to watch everyone, her camera hanging from her neck by an adjustable leather strap. She reminded herself, based on Lila's input, of their unique connections with the bride and groom and then snapped a few candid shots, wishing her aunt and uncle would arrive to help her identify people and make introductions.

Two middle-aged men walked in separately, one resembling Lila. Eleanor surmised he was the beloved Arthur, Lila's first cousin who now lived with the Stoffs after spending nearly a decade in Shanghai. The other man had a woman at his arm. Eleanor overheard him talking and deduced he was American-born and had to be the famous John Brandeis. Their "savior," as Lila put it.

Next, two couples arrived, each with a child in tow. A bouncy girl, freckled, her red hair in ringlets, skipped ahead of her parents. Eleanor thought her to be five or six. She had to be Franny, her parents Tasa's aunt Norah and uncle Levi. Norah Eisen was Halina's sister. She and Levi were the ones who had fixed Tasa up with Eli not even a year earlier. Eli had worked part-time for Levi while he was finishing college on the GI Bill. They thought he'd be perfect for their niece, who'd just arrived by boat, having survived the war. Norah and Levi drove to Atlantic City and brought Tasa back to live with them in Columbus. A babysitter for Franny and a date for Eli. And today, a bride. Pretty clever, Eleanor decided.

The other couple had a young son who looked to be nine or ten. She figured this had to be Lila's childhood friend, Zelda Muni, with her husband Giorgio. She remembered Lila telling her the boy's name was Umberto. Eleanor could hardly believe the heartwarming stories surrounding this couple who had immigrated to New York shortly before the Depression. Apparently, Zelda had single-handedly convinced John Brandeis to sponsor Lila, Bart, and Eli when Germany took over Austria. Zelda had no previous connection with Brandeis, just her chutzpah and resourcefulness in finding a wealthy Jewish philanthropist willing to take responsibility for three immigrants he didn't know. This part of the family's lore seemed to Eleanor nothing short of a miracle.

So much serendipity and luck, purpose and resilience. It suddenly occurred to her that a photo essay about this family could be a charming story, one that might captivate a nation getting past a world war. If only they'd grant her permission.

∞∞∞

FACING RABBI ZELKOWITZ, Eli and Tasa stood side by side, their hands tightly clasped, under a simple linen chuppah in the temple's small chapel. A sheer nylon veil covered Tasa's face, held on by a headband covered in delicate daisies. Her thick black hair, pulled behind her ears, hung down her back, smoothed under at the bottom. A delicate corsage of pink roses accented her jacket, a similar spray of flowers worn by her mother and aunt. Eli, like all the men, wore a simple white carnation on his lapel.

Lily, Bart, Halina, and Salomon each held one of the four poles that supported the canopy. They stood before a room full of guests, all seated in wooden folding chairs, the men in their best suits—single- and double-breasted with stylish ties—the women in silk blouses and velvet skirts, flowered dresses, or tailored dress suits. The women grasped their husbands' hands or held white handkerchiefs tight in anticipation.

The rabbi murmured his initial words, clearly intending them only for Tasa and Eli. Eleanor's lens captured their clasped hands, and then she drew back the camera's focus as Rabbi Zelkowitz pronounced the ancient and binding vow that Eli and Tasa repeated, "*Ani ledodi vedodi li*"—"I am my beloved's, and my beloved is mine." Her camera clicked as they stared into each other's eyes when the rabbi pronounced them man and wife. As they kissed, cheers of "*Mazel tov!*" erupted. The couple pulled apart, Tasa blushing, taking hold of Eli's hand. *Click.*

Rabbi Zelkowitz spoke directly to the congregation. "In our tradition, even the most joyous moment cannot exist without a thought of something painful shattering the happiness like fragile glass." He placed a linen-wrapped glass beneath Eli's feet. Eleanor caught a clear view of Eli's face just then, absorbed in this significant act. As he stomped on the symbolic token, she took her shot. More cheers of "*Mazel tov!*"

Each guest in the receiving line held Tasa, then Eli, in an emotional hug, their eyes moist as they congratulated the newlyweds. Eleanor snapped pictures of the wedding onlookers as she unobtrusively made her way around the room. *Being a photographer is observing so much of life's ups and downs,* she thought. *It is the joy that is harder to hold tight than the sorrow.*

As the wedding party and their guests moved from the chapel to the adjacent social hall, Eleanor motioned for Eli's Army friends to pose with the groom. Four men in their midtwenties who could pass for brothers appeared in her viewfinder. They wore similar double-breasted suits and cuffed pants, all devilishly handsome with dark wavy hair and bad-boy grins. She couldn't help smiling as she thought of all the tricks and secrets these soldiers must have shared during their brief but intense stint together in wartime.

Eli was approached by John Brandeis, leaving Eleanor with Eli's three friends.

"You're the photojournalist with the *Plain Dealer*. Eleanor Weiss, right? I'm Henry White." Henry held out his hand while Eleanor let her camera hang at her waist, thankful the neck strap kept moments like these from being awkward. "Meet my buddies Max Schultz and Bobby Saltman."

She noticed Max held a trumpet and Bobby a harmonica. "Nice to directly meet all of you. But you're not part of the band, are you?" She looked across the room to where an instrumental group—a violinist, a bassist, a saxophonist, and a singer—was setting up.

"We told Eli we wanted to play at his wedding. He heard enough of us over the nights at Camp Ritchie. Music was our emotional safety zone." Max toyed with his tuning slide as he spoke. "We practiced last night with this group and again a few hours ago so we could hold our own. Right, Bobby?"

"Yep. But we gotta go over now. Nice meeting you, Miss Weiss."

As Max and Bobby hurried off, Henry stayed put. Eleanor detected slight German accents in all of the Ritchie boys except Henry. "We could be relatives, you know?" Henry offered. When she responded with a puzzled look, he quickly added, "My parents changed our name from Weiss to White when they came over from Berlin after the Great War. I grew up in Queens. Tough neighborhood, pretty anti-Semitic. Name change never protected me."

Eleanor hadn't felt discrimination growing up in Cleveland, but she was also almost fifteen years older than Henry, and the times had been different then. She may have been one of very few Jewish students at the University of Missouri, and she ran around with students like herself—single-minded about learning everything there was to know about photography. Her job at the paper was similarly secular in nature. As she was about to reply, the musicians began tuning their instruments, and she excused herself to get back to work.

She moved toward the center of the room and snapped a photograph just as Tasa and Eli strode onto the dance floor. She captured the split second the musicians nodded to each other and began playing "Until," a song the singer announced was picked by Eli for the occasion. It was one Eleanor had heard Tommy Dorsey sing. She snapped the loving family and friends standing close around them. She wished she could record the words that melted into the intimate space as the lovers, now husband and wife, held each other close.

You were sent from heaven just for me, and you are oh so heavenly. Until there is no moon above, there's no such thing as love, I'll love but you.

Everyone clapped as the band segued into Tasa's pick. Eleanor recognized "It's Magic," from the film *Romance on the High Seas* that she saw last year, sung by a new actress named Doris Day.

You sigh, the song begins. You speak and I hear violins. It's magic. . . . When I am in your arms,

when we walk hand in hand, the world becomes a
wonderland. It's magic.
    How else can I explain those rainbows when
there is no rain. It's magic.
    Why do I tell myself these things that happen
are all really true when in my heart I know the magic
is my love for you?

She felt a hand on her arm and turned to face Henry White again. "You gotta join me in at least one dance." He lifted Eleanor's camera over her head, still connected by her neck strap, placed it on an empty table, and whisked her onto the dance floor, but only after she had snapped shots of the six couples doing a fox-trot alongside the newlyweds: both sets of proud parents, along with the Eisens, the Munis, Emma and Simon Goldstein, and Hershel and Rebecca.

As Henry spun Eleanor on the floor, she reminded him she was nearly old enough to be his mother while silently admiring his youthful charm and confidence. As the band paused between songs, the dancers dispersed. Eleanor grabbed her camera and moved around the social hall. She wanted to capture all the connections and gestures and love in the room. As the band resumed with a jazzy Benny Goodman number, she watched nine-year-old Umberto Muni pulling five-year-old Franny Eisen around the dance floor, their respective parents giggling as they looked on. *Click.* Arthur Zeidl and John Brandeis were engrossed in conversation, first serious, then breaking into laughter. Brandeis's gold watch chain sparkled in the light coming through the west window just as he appeared to be looking straight through her camera in pure glee. *Click.*

The music got louder as Tasa and Eli were pushed toward the center of the floor, the crowd tightly surrounding them, clapping wildly.

∞

A STRETCH OF DANCING consumed the celebrants until, finally, the crowd seemed to catch their collective breaths and the two sets of parents stepped to the center of the room to speak. Lila gestured for Halina and Salomon, as the bride's parents, to offer the first toast. Salomon took his wife's hand and cleared his throat.

"Halina and I were separated for five years during the war. The Soviets had deported her to Siberia. Neither of us knew the other was alive, but we never lost our love or our hope." Salomon locked eyes with Halina, then turned back to the onlookers. "We wish for Tasa and Eli a love that withstands all of life's challenges, and a life whose challenges are bearable." The crowd lifted their glasses and, in unison, cried "*L'Chaim!*"

Lila moved forward, her arm in Bart's. "Family is what is most important, what is most valuable." She nodded toward her cousin Arthur. "Arthur and I—our mothers were twin sisters—so we grew up very close. Arthur left Vienna for Shanghai, and a short time later, Bart and I escaped with Eli to America. Despite ten years of separation, we've resumed our close relationship. And Bart and I have found a family in the friends we've made in Columbus." Lila turned to Bart, raising her glass. "We wish for Tasa and Eli to always be surrounded by family and friends."

Bart nodded in agreement and spoke slowly. "Nothing ever stopped Eli. He adjusted to whatever life handed him. Eli turns lemons into lemonade." The cliché mixed with Bart's heavy accent and broken English brought on much laughter. "I wish for Eli and Tasa that this will always be how they approach life's *Kampfe.*" He looked to Lila and she translated—"struggles"— just as Eleanor snapped another shot.

With the toasts finished, everyone crowded the bountiful buffet table—covered by platters of brisket, lox, potato latkes, steamed cabbage, macaroni salad, and loaf after loaf of challah. When it was time for the cake, Eli and Tasa walked to the table displaying the multi-layered creation. Tasa looked over at Halina, who nodded for her to go ahead. Eleanor snapped their moment of hesitation, and again snapped the instant Tasa slid a knife into the yellow-iced, chocolate indulgence. She focused on Tasa's face through her viewfinder and snapped just as Tasa pursed her lips while forking a large piece into Eli's mouth.

As slices of cake were distributed, the music rose again in the background. Eleanor snapped a shot of Max on trumpet and Bobby on harmonica right before the singer joined in, her voice full, crooning the lyrics to Sinatra's "But None Like You."

The world is full of people, but none like you. They're ordinary people, but none like you. How far away is yesterday before you came along . . .

It was time for Tasa and Eli to speak. Eli nodded to Tasa, and it became clear who would address their family and friends first. With her arm tightly coiled inside Eli's elbow, Tasa began. "Make no mistake. This fix-up by Aunt Norah and Uncle Levi last September was obvious to me, but I ignored it. At first." She turned toward Eli. "Boy, this has been a whirlwind affair!" Laughter erupted.

"As I was saying, they certainly didn't drive halfway across the country just to say hello. And let's hope they could have found a babysitter within this wonderful Columbus community to watch Franny without bringing me back with them. But I was ready for a change and welcomed the chance to attend university again." She paused and gulped in a breath before continuing. "Then, the moment I met Eli, just days after

I arrived, I knew." Her voice cracked as she turned to Eli. Eleanor was aware that Tasa had had a love affair during the war—Lila had told her Tasa planned to marry the young man, but he was killed in the Battle of Berlin. Tasa choked out her next words. "I never thought I'd fall in love again."

Eleanor's camera caught Eli's eyes, glued to Tasa as she spoke, and then again when he tenderly reached for her. Following the brief murmurs and chants of "*L'Chaim*," Eli stepped forward. He began by tracing his life from Vienna to New York to Columbus, to wartime, and back to Columbus to meet the love of his life.

"I've been lucky in my life so far to have such strong relationships. First and foremost, with my family and extended family and those no longer with us. But even as a tormented kid in Vienna, I had a friend, a non-Jewish boy who stood up for me at every turn, even at his own peril. My only regret is that Toby was left in Vienna, likely with no choice but to fight with the German forces, something he would have found abhorrent." He paused, his eyes becoming glassy. Eleanor clicked.

"When my family moved to Columbus, we were taken in by the Goldsteins—generous and loving people—and I was lucky to gain another wonderful friend, Hershel." Eli paused, his eyes singling Hershel out from the crowd. "He taught me everything I know today."

There was laughter, with Hershel calling back, "I would say the same of you, Eli!" Eli beamed as he shared how the two would go to the movies so he could improve his English, and to get a better sense of the colloquialisms. "I know my mother's Viennese baking helped me make and keep lots of friends." More laughter, more shutter clicks.

Eli spoke about the confidence he gained as an American soldier, which taught him he could face tough situations; that he had the good fortune to see places and form bonds with people he would never have met otherwise, "some of whom I was thrown together with at Camp Ritchie and are with us today." All eyes went toward Max, Henry, and Bobby. "I was proud I could serve the United States in the capacity I did. America gave me my freedom, thanks to several here today . . ." Zelda and Giorgio Muni stood with John Brandeis and his wife, and all eyes, grateful eyes, took them in, as did Eleanor's camera. "I was able to give back by fighting for that freedom.

"Much of what happened in my life, like that of my family and Tasa and her family, came from factors outside my control. Today is different. Tasa is the person I choose to spend the rest of my life with, the one I want to plan my world around."

∞∞∞

THE BLACK-AND-WHITE photograph, at first glance, reveals a young couple in their midtwenties. She wears a white short-sleeved, round-collared knit top and shorts, and she clutches a purse. He sports an open-collared light shirt, the sleeves rolled above his elbows, dark slacks. The woman semi-reclines amid blades of grass and ferns, her right arm molding around the man's left knee. Her dark, peaceful eyes gaze directly into the camera, her full lips turn slightly upward. The man kneels behind her, his eyes cast on her face, his arm tenderly around her shoulder, blanketed by a lock of her black hair as he cups her ear in his hand. His other arm rests along his right thigh, his fingers curling under the knee he plants on the ground. There's a harmony to the couple's pose, like birds singing side by side on a sturdy tree branch. A slight shadow throws its image across their exposed skin from the ferns and shrubs that surround them. Their heads tilt left, their faces parallel, hers just below his.

Eleanor's eyes lingered on her composition a few moments longer. She'd shot it the day after Tasa and Eli's wedding. It was part of a series she sold to *Life* magazine, with the blessings of all involved.

By then, she'd understood how serendipitous their union actually was. Two young European immigrants, each from a different country—those countries fighting the same enemy—who found one another in the middle of America. But the essence of her photo narrative was an American soldier who had grown up in Vienna, escaped persecution thanks to someone who vouched for his family, and returned to the theater of war to fight for his new country. She included many candid shots of the four Camp Ritchie boys from the wedding but was able to contrast those with a few Eli had provided of them in uniform. The coda of her series was how the soldier came back home to find the love of his life, and how both—Eli and Tasa—set down the roots for the future they'd lost in childhood. Reflected in this final photograph.

She shuffled through several pictures she hadn't included in the spread for the magazine. There was the moment after they were pronounced man and wife, when Tasa took hold of Eli's hand. The one where Eli and Tasa strode for the first time onto the dance floor together. That shot of Tasa pursing her lips while forking a big bite of cake into Eli's open mouth.

She paused at one particular photograph, a lump rising in her throat. There it was. The crisp image of Eli the instant he stomped on a linen-wrapped glass, Tasa and the two sets of parents watching intently in the background, both joy and suffering, in equal measures, etching their faces.

AUTHOR'S NOTE

ONE AFTERNOON IN 2014, as I sat on the couch in my parents' apartment, my dad handed me a letter. I opened the folded sheet and stopped at the salutation.

"Why did they call you a Ritchie Boy?" I asked.

"You knew I trained at Camp Ritchie," he reminded me.

Of course, I did. As a trained journalist, I had recorded the rich family history from both my immigrant parents decades earlier: my mother growing up in eastern Poland, my father in Vienna. I knew so much but never made the connection that my father's training at Camp Ritchie in Maryland meant there was a name for him: that he was a Ritchie Boy, one of thousands of young, mostly Jewish men who understood the German language and culture, who were recruited to train at Camp Ritchie where the US Army centralized its intelligence operations, and who worked undercover on the European front to help the Allies win World War II.

After I read that letter and realized my dad was part of something much bigger, I immediately began to research online and found a documentary about the Ritchie Boys. I watched it with my dad. It drove home to me what these young men were giving back to their newly adopted country and how indebted we are to them. I also began to think about the touchpoints my dad had shared with me decades earlier. About his journey from one homeland to another. About his journey from boyhood to manhood.

So, while *A Ritchie Boy*, which begins in 1938, is about a Jewish soldier named Eli Stoff fighting in World War II, it's also about the circumstances and people Eli encounters: from Vienna to New York, from Ohio to Maryland, and from a Paris suburb called Le Vésinet in the midst of war to the Midwest, where Eli returns to set down his roots.

A Ritchie Boy is an immigrant story, a family drama rooted in persecution, and a human narrative about this powerful network of Jewish soldiers, most no longer living but each given a special name.

My father is the inspiration for this fictional story. He, too, grew up in anti-Semitic Vienna in the 1920s and '30s, was a teenage immigrant adjusting to life in the Midwest as World War II began, and became a young man recruited and trained by the US Army as a military intelligence officer fighting the very enemy he barely escaped in 1938. His journey, and that of the fictional Eli Stoff, represents thousands who have arrived on our shores, and continue to arrive, as they contribute to our collective freedoms.

Indeed, I am thankful to all those who sacrificed for our country. And I am deeply grateful to my parents and grandparents of blessed memory. I have kept them alive in my memories and in the stories I tell.

My gratitude extends to many others.

To my husband, Frank, my first reader and biggest advocate. I am so lucky to have a partner so steadfast and encouraging of my writing.

To Ellen Lesser whose expert guidance and encouragement over the years helped me become a better novelist. I am also grateful to Matt Bondurant, Tom Jenks, and the late Lee K. Abbott for valuable feedback during early workshops of stories in *A Ritchie Boy*. To my beta readers Davi Blake, Nick Breyfogle, Carole Gerber, Joy Gonsiorowski, Pat Losinski, Leann Schneider, Richard VanGuilder, and Alec Wightman for their commitment of time and thoughtful feedback.

I wish to acknowledge OSU Libraries Reference Archivist Michelle Drobik. Her helpful assistance led me to a trove of historic photographs and documents that immeasurably added to my rich understanding of campus life at Ohio State University in the 1940s as the country prepared for war, and at the time when protagonist Eli Stoff attended college there. In addition, OSU Eastern European scholar Nick Breyfogle was always willing to take my calls to verify particular facts of the broader history of the World War II era.

I so appreciate the capable team at She Writes Press led by Brooke Warner, and all the talented professionals who played a role in transforming *A Ritchie Boy* from manuscript to the book you now hold. Many thanks to Barrett Briske, Katie Caruana, Krissa Lagos, Tabitha Lahr, Julie Metz, and my diligent editorial manager Lauren Wise. Heartfelt thanks to my publicist Caitlin Hamilton Summie, and to Bryan Azorsky, Alex Baker, Lucinda Dyer, and Libby Jordan.

I am deeply grateful to those who took the time to read my manuscript and endorse it: Nina Barrett, Jennifer Chiaverini, Fiona Davis, Alex George, Kristin Harmel, Pamela Klinger-Horn, Julia Keller, Pat Losinski, Lee Martin, Stewart O'Nan, Helen Schulman, and Linda White.

My love and gratefulness to my extraordinary family, and family of friends, whose support I treasure every day.

To the memory of my Vienna-born father, Ernest Stern, to whom this novel is dedicated. His role as a Ritchie Boy, and the details of his early life, sparked this work of fiction.

READER'S GUIDE

1. Why do you think the author told the novel in stories? What do the stories allow that a novel told in traditional form would not? Have you read other novels with this structure?

2. Eli and his parents were lucky to escape Austria. How else does luck play a role in this novel?

3. Did you know about the Ritchie Boys prior to reading this novel? If not, were you surprised to learn that there is still history about World War II that is not widely known?

4. This novel is inspired by the author's father's life. Kass wrote an earlier novel inspired by her mother's life. If you have not already done so, will you now go read *Tasa's Song*? If you have read *Tasa's Song*, how do the two work together?

5. This novel is about family: the family one has and the family one creates. Discuss.

6. The Ritchie Boys were heroes. Does this novel have other heroes? How do you define a hero?

7. Although the experience as a Ritchie Boy was formative, Eli didn't talk much about it after the war. Indeed, there were pictures of his time at Camp Ritchie with people his daughter did not know. Why do you think such a powerful experience was left, by and large, unexpressed?

8. This is an immigrant story, and there are many immigrant stories. How is this novel similar to other immigrant stories you've read? How is it different?

9. How does this novel portray friendships? Why are friend-ships pivotal to the narrative?

10. Place is important in this book. In what ways does the author tell her story by describing Austria, New York, Columbus, Camp Ritchie, and Le Vésinet?

CREDITS

ABOUT THE AUTHOR

LINDA KASS began her career as a magazine writer and correspondent for regional and national publications. Her work has previously appeared in *TIME*, the *Detroit Free Press, Columbus Monthly,* and, more recently, *Full Grown People, The MacGuffin,* and *Kenyon Review Online.* She is the author of the historical World War II novel *Tasa's Song* (2016) and is the founder and owner of Gramercy Books, an independent bookstore in central Ohio.

lindakass.com

SELECTED TITLES FROM SHE WRITES PRESS

She Writes Press is an independent publishing company founded to serve women writers everywhere. Visit us at www.shewritespress.com.

An Address in Amsterdam by Mary Dingee Fillmore. $16.95, 978-1-63152-133-1. After facing relentless danger and escalating raids for 18 months, Rachel Klein—a well-behaved young Jewish woman who transformed herself into a courier for the underground when the Nazis invaded her country—persuades her parents to hide with her in a dank basement, where much is revealed.

Don't Put the Boats Away by Ames Sheldon. $16.95, 978-1-63152-602-2. In the aftermath of World War II, the members of the Sutton family are reeling from the death of their "golden boy," Eddie. Over the next twenty-five years, they all struggle with loss, grief, and mourning—and pay high prices, including divorce and alcoholism.

Tasa's Song by Linda Kass. $16.95, 978-1-63152-064-8. From a peaceful village in eastern Poland to a partitioned post-war Vienna, from a promising childhood to a year living underground, Tasa's Song celebrates the bonds of love, the power of memory, the solace of music, and the enduring strength of the human spirit.

Even in Darkness by Barbara Stark-Nemon. $16.95, 978-1-63152-956-6. From privileged young German-Jewish woman to concentration camp refugee, Kläre Kohler navigates the horrors of war and—through unlikely sources—finds the strength, hope, and love she needs to survive.

Bess and Frima by Alice Rosenthal. $16.95, 978-1-63152-439-4. Bess and Frima, best friends from the Bronx, find romance at their summer jobs at Jewish vacation hotels in the Catskills—and as love mixes with war, politics, creative ambitions, and the mysteries of personality, they leave girlhood behind them.